PROMISE BOYS

PROMISE BOYS

NICK BROOKS

H

HENRY HOLT AND COMPANY

New York

Henry Holt and Company, *Publishers since 1866*
Henry Holt® is a registered trademark of Macmillan Publishing Group, LLC
120 Broadway, New York, NY 10271 • fiercereads.com

Our books may be purchased in bulk for promotional, educational, or business use.
Please contact your local bookseller or the Macmillan Corporate and Premium Sales Department at
(800) 221-7945 ext. 5442 or by email at MacmillanSpecialMarkets@macmillan.com.

Library of Congress Cataloging-in-Publication Data is available.

First edition, 2023
Book design by Michelle Gengaro-Kokmen
Printed in the United States of America

ISBN 978-1-250-86697-4 (hardcover)
1   3   5   7   9   10   8   6   4   2

Created in association with Cake Creative LLC

To the boys of Chocolate City

I've noticed a fascinating phenomenon in my twenty-five years of teaching—that schools and schooling are increasingly irrelevant to the great enterprises of the planet. No one believes anymore that scientists are trained in science classes or politicians in civics classes or poets in English classes. The truth is that schools don't really teach anything except how to obey orders. This is a great mystery to me because thousands of humane, caring people work in schools as teachers and aides and administrators, but the abstract logic of the institution overwhelms their individual contributions. Although teachers do care and do work very hard, the institution is psychopathic—it has no conscience.

It rings a bell and the young man in the middle of writing a poem must close his notebook and move to [a] different cell where he must memorize that man and monkeys derive from a common ancestor.

—John Taylor Gatto
"Why Schools Don't Educate"

BREAKING NEWS:

BELOVED PRINCIPAL KILLED AT 43

DC police are investigating a homicide in Northeast DC. Mr. Kenneth Moore, founder and principal of Urban Promise Prep, was shot to death on school premises on Friday, October 10. He was a beloved member of the community.

A coworker found Moore's body early Friday evening and called 911.

When officers arrived, they discovered Moore with a single gunshot wound to the temple. He was pronounced dead on the scene.

Detectives have been working to establish a suspect or suspects and motive in this case, and it's reported they have already detained three students for questioning.

Anyone with information is asked to call the District of Columbia Police Department's Homicide Unit at 202-555-4925.

A reward of up to $65,000 is offered to anyone who provides information leading to an arrest and indictment in this case.

PART ONE

J.B.

Present Day

Nobody
Urban Promise Prep Student

Rumor has it a student brought a gun to school the day of the murder. You didn't hear that from me.

Keyana Glenn

Anacostia High School Student

We can't believe the things we see, we can only believe the things we feel. I thought I could believe in J.B. because I could feel how much he liked me. Or at least I thought I could, until he stood me up. The day after we got so close. When he had told me he'd meet me after school and we'd go to the game together. That we'd *be* together. Officially.

He swore he was different. Not like other guys. Better than them. And against my gut feeling, he convinced me to trust him. And maybe I still do? But my head's a mess and I don't know anything right now.

Agh, I feel like such a fool. I got used, or tricked. Now I feel bad about *myself*, and that ain't fair. Even thinking about it pisses me off.

Every time I close my eyes, the night plays over and over again. Me dragging myself to the game all alone, ready to confront J.B. But when I arrived, I saw him covered in blood.

I froze right there in the school doorway.

We both did.

Everything I'd wanted to scream at him bubbled up, getting stuck in my mouth.

The blood.

My thoughts raced. Did he get hurt? Was that the reason he hadn't picked me up like he said he would? Is that why he hadn't called or texted me back?

"It wasn't my fault . . . ," he whispered while trying to catch his breath. He then took off. He clearly wasn't injured, not moving that fast.

He disappeared into the darkness of the evening.

Of course, at the time I didn't know about Principal Moore. Everyone's saying J.B. killed that man, but I mean, part of me can't believe that.

On the other hand, I know what I saw, J.B. with blood all over his shirt and his words replaying over and over again in my head. "It wasn't my fault."

Every time I start to believe in something, I'm reminded that *everyone* around here is so fake. I guess you never truly know a person.

I hope I'm wrong. I hope J.B. is innocent.

Nurse Robin

Urban Promise Prep Employee

Don't get me wrong, I care about the work. It's this *place* that I can't stand.

When I told my friends I'd be working at Urban Promise Prep, they all warned me about it being all male, but I figured I could handle it. I have to deal with nasty men twenty-four hours a day. Every school I've worked at, every bus ride, every stroll down the street, every grocery trip, men hit on me. Why would Promise Prep be any different? Right?

Wrong.

At Urban Promise, I was incredibly uncomfortable, *nervous*; you know the feeling. Principal Moore created a boiling pot of toxic masculinity and male fragility. You think I'm talking about the students, but no. The kids are kids, they don't know any better. It's the adults. The teachers, the security guards, the leadership.

They encouraged the behavior. Last year, a boy circulated some inappropriate video he made with a young girl so the security guards searched his things and confiscated his phone. It was the right thing to do. But he never actually got detention or suspension. Not even a slap on the wrist! And worse, I saw the guards in the break room passing around the dang phone, watching the thing before they deleted it. Snickering over literal child pornography, cracking jokes about the young lady in the video. They didn't even think twice. Just no sense of . . . morality when it came to women at Urban Promise.

But Moore didn't care about that. As long as the boys were in line, these men could act a fool. You know, Moore is so pristine in the public eye, but he wasn't squeaky clean either. He did the little things like hug me too long or put his hand on the small of my back when he spoke to me in the hall.

Also, call me ridiculous or whatever, but I swear he had an alcohol problem. I've treated plenty of patients with drinking habits and Moore fit the bill. His mood would change at the drop of a dime. Sometimes smooth as silk, charming and gregarious, supportive and kind. Then other times, I've seen him snap at kids, snap at teachers, even snap at Dean Hicks. And lately, it'd been worse than usual.

Anyway. Guess you could say I don't think it's as much of a loss as other people do.

As far as the boys they're questioning about his murder, I didn't really know them, but I did see J.B. the day of the shooting. He came to me to get his hand bandaged. He scraped it pretty bad after punching something.

"What happened?" I asked him. His fists were clenched tight, like he was trying to dig his nails into his own skin. The deep brown of it threaded with blood.

"Nothing," he mumbled.

"Can't be nothing if you're here with your hand looking like this." I tried to smile at him, make him more comfortable since his knuckles were so shredded.

I did my best to clean the wound, but he wouldn't loosen his hand. Not the entire time he sat in the office. He just glared off into the distance, jaw clenched, like he couldn't wait to do something more with that messed-up fist.

I walked backward to my desk before telling him he could leave. A weird instinct came over me. I didn't want to turn my back to him. Not with the anger radiating off him like heat. Like he could swing again at any moment, his hands needing a punching bag, something, anything to connect with in this moment. That's someone who is accustomed to violence. At that young age? Makes me shudder.

So, yeah. I'm looking for a new school to work at.

Becca Buckingham

Mercy Academy for Girls Student

Those poor boys. So full of anger. It's because of their life circumstances though, right? I mean, imagine if you lived in poverty, were racially profiled, and a victim of systemic inequity. You would be too. That's why I choose to tutor at Promise. To make a *difference*. With my white privilege, I see it as my responsibility.

But even with all that, I can't bring myself to understand why they'd kill Principal Moore. Especially after all he's done for them. It's just a tragedy.

They say they have three suspects. Everyone's been talking and DC is smaller than you think. Word travels fast. I actually tutored one of them.

Ramón Zambrano.

Ramón is just the nicest kid. There's something . . . angelic about him. I love how, like, authentic he is about his culture. Making . . . I think it's called pahpooses? The little biscuit things. I heard he makes them with his grandma. How sweet is that?

I went into overdrive trying to get him fluent in English because it'd help land him more opportunities. Not to mention it was my duty. And Ramón really took to it. In fact, a few weeks ago, I would've said there's no way he did this. And a part of me still feels that in my heart. Though I saw . . . um, let's just say I *heard* he can have a temper.

But there's hope for him. It's probably one of the other boys they arrested.

Like . . . **Trey Jackson.**

I never actually spoke to him. But I heard he was funny. A lot of the girls at Mercy thought he was hot, plus he plays basketball, so you know. He might grow up and be in the NBA—who wouldn't want to date that guy?

Me.

Athletes are douchebags and I'm sure Trey's no different. Come to think of it, people called him a bully. He'd crack jokes on kids all the time, making himself feel big by making others feel small.

But people also said he has, like, a military uncle with a bad attitude. Sometimes guys who have mean father figures turn out mean too, you know? At least he *has* a father figure, though! I don't know for sure, but I bet that's not very common with the boys at this school.

And then there's J.B. Williamson.

I don't know him any better than Trey, but I hear J.B. is pretty smart. I saw him a lot in the halls on tutoring days, and I mainly remembered him because he's huge. Like 6′3″! Which, tall guys are always sexy to me. But he never smiled. No matter how many times I smiled at him or said hi, he would just ignore me. That kind of gave me a weird feeling, you know?

Everyone keeps asking me about *that* day at Promise. I'd been tutoring all afternoon in the ESL room. I'd stepped out to grab water and there they were: J.B. and Principal Moore in a fight.

I froze in place along with everyone else. J.B. towered over Principal Moore, and there was a massive dent left behind in a locker. The tattered skin of J.B.'s knuckles bled on the linoleum floor. I felt the tension from across the hall.

J.B. bucked at Principal Moore, waiting for him to flinch or cower. But Principal Moore laughed, standing his ground. My heart rattled in my chest and my pulse thundered so loud I didn't catch most of the argument.

Principal Moore put his hand in the air, directing J.B. to walk away, and as J.B. stomped past me all aggressive and angry, I heard him mumble, "I'mma see you."

I'd heard boys at Promise say that before. Seemed like the last straw in a fight. As school security officers would pry them apart, they'd shout the phrase at each other over and over again. A warning. And without a doubt, later the gossip would travel to Mercy about the fights in the neighborhood with the Promise boys.

But now, those three words echo in my head on repeat. A few hours after J.B. uttered them, Principal Moore turned up dead.

Unk

Neighborhood Dude

I don't care about no damn principal.

Principal don't care about me.

Huh?!

That man never even looked me in my face, like I ain't exist.

Only time he spoke to me was to yell at me to leave from around his school.

I'm from here. I was here first! *Whatyoutalmbout*!

Uppity-ass Black folks taking over just like white folks.

WELCOME TO THE DISTRICT, BABY. HAHAHAHAA!

You see where I'm at!!

LONG LIVE CHOCOLATE CITY!!!!

Wilson Hicks

Urban Promise Prep Dean of the Student Body

Oh God.

I found him dead.

Oh God, why'd it have to be me?

I've never seen blood move like that. A red river rushing along the edges of the desk.

Blank eyes stared back.

I stepped closer and closer. "Kenneth! Kenneth!"

My eyes scanned over his body. I couldn't tell where the blood came from. I covered my nose because the smell of feces in the air gave the death away. Kenneth had shit himself. I'd always heard that people shit themselves when they die, but thought it was nothing more than just a myth.

I scrambled backward. I felt my face go red. Sweat poured down my temples. Questions raced through my head: What were those final moments like? How afraid had he been when the trigger was pulled? Did he feel much pain? Was he afraid to die?

But I'll never have answers to those questions.

Even now, when that night starts playing over again in my head, it all comes rushing back. Could I have done something differently? Could I have prevented this from happening?

Were we best friends? No. Technically, he was my boss. But when Kenneth set out to create Urban Promise Prep, he hired me first, and together, we built something truly remarkable. Say what you want about his methods, or mine even, but we got results. Sure, we showed the kids tough love but we never crossed the line. We cared about these boys more than most, and all we wanted was the best for them. We wanted to make them into kings. We even founded the Promise Fund, a scholarship to send kids to college if they couldn't afford it themselves. But some people couldn't see that we were in the business of building men, not coddling boys.

Unfortunately, some students just refuse to grow up.

J.B. Williamson, Ramón Zambrano, and Trey Jackson, all boys who refuse to grow up.

One of them did this, maybe all of them together. The records show the three of them had spats with Kenneth that day.

If I had to put money on it, J.B. did this. It's always the quiet ones you have to worry about. The ones swallowing down their violent streak. Plus, J.B.'s from Benning Terrace. I've seen his kind time and time again. You know the type of kids who come out of there.

Bando

Neighborhood Hustler

Kill, moe! I'd just seen my man too! Now they're saying he might get booked for a murder rap? J.B. never really kicked it on the block like that. I mean, he be outside, but he wasn't hustling or nothing. He always seemed like a good kid. I do know that man had hands, though. If pushed, he could fight and land you in the hospital if you come into contact with one of his fists.

{inhale}

I remember one time at the rec we were hooping, and J.B. hung around the courts chilling. He's big as hell so you'd think he'd be a beast at basketball, but come to find out, he don't ball. Anyway, we needed a fifth man to play so I convinced him to join the game. And for a while, he was hanging in there, but because of his size, they kept hacking my man. Every time he'd try to drive, they'd hack him. Slapping the shit out of his arms trying to get the ball and make him look like a clown.

J.B. cool, though, he never really wanted smoke, just wanted to get along. But he had his limits like anyone. So, when they peeped he's not that aggressive, they started hacking my man even more! One dude caught J.B. with an elbow and out of nowhere, J.B. decked my man with the meanest right hook I've ever seen. It was almost like a reflex. Blood went everywhere. Broke that man's nose and dude went out cold, hit the ground before J.B. even realized what he did.

{*exhale*}

But even with that, I definitely never saw him as no killer.

{*inhale*}

But then again, I know a lotta dudes who weren't killers until they killed. Young as fourteen, moe. You know, sometimes that shit just lurks in you until the right moment comes along.

{*exhale*}

I guess it's possible. Maybe J.B. did do that shit. Maybe his anger brought it out.

Mr. Reggie

Urban Promise Prep School Resource Officer

Detention's always light on game days. Especially *that* day. The play-offs, I think. These boys already get it so hard at Urban Promise Prep: no talking, no laughing, *no girls*. Their only outlet really is our basketball team.

Anybody's allowed to come watch the games and we're actually pretty good this year, so girls from all across the city come to see the boys play. They love that. Which is why I thought I'd be able to skip detention duty and leave work early for a change, but turns out there were still a few kids who decided to get in some trouble: J.B., Ramón, and Trey.

J.B. arrived first, and I have to be honest, it had me shocked. In my six years at Urban Promise, I can confidently say that I've never seen J.B. Williamson in after-school detention. Quiet kid, big as hell, but a soft demeanor.

Ramón rolled in next. He stayed in and out of detention, usually because he was caught shooting dice or skipping class, nothing major. The usual. Stupid kid stuff. I liked that about him, he had spunk. He'd march in, primping that slick hair of his with a brush, and reminding me of the Fonz. Whenever he saw me, he'd say, "Hey, Mister, how those Ravens doing?" after spotting my Baltimore Ravens mug one time.

"We're looking good," I'd always reply, whether it was true or not.

He didn't care about them, but he knew to be on my good side in case he ended up in detention later that day. He was smart like that. Manipulative even. But sweet.

So sure enough that day, Ramón sauntered into detention asking me about the Ravens. He gritted his teeth, a little on edge. He's not usually an angry kid, but I could tell something was eating him. I asked him if he needed to talk, but he just shrugged me off, mean-mugging. But I could handle him—angry as he was, it was just Ramón.

Even with his bad attitude, I still thought this would be a pretty light detention, until . . . in walked Trey Jackson. Trey ALWAYS lived in here. We butted heads all day, every day. Though he acted like it was funny. Some sort of game he played with all of us school resource officers.

So that day, Trey kept asking to go to the bathroom, over and over and over and over. Kid must've thought I was dumb! He and I both knew he just wanted to go to the gym to check out the basketball game. And even still, Trey pressed my buttons so much, incessantly raising his hand and sucking his teeth every few seconds, that I just let him go.

At first I didn't think anything of it, but after a good amount of time passed, I realized I needed to go check on him. With only J.B. and Ramón left behind, I figured, they're good enough kids, things would be okay. They'd stay put, follow the rules, and be done with detention.

I looked all over the school and came up empty.

I never found Trey.

But then I heard the *Bang*. The school went wild. Screams filled the hallways. The gym erupted. I ran with the other school resource officers toward the sound of gunfire. I tailed them back near the detention room.

When we barreled in, J.B. and Ramón were gone. Dean Hicks yelled for help next door, and that's when we saw that Principal Moore had been shot. We called the ambulance immediately and tried to keep people out of the way.

In all my years as a school resource officer, I've never given in to the kids, and the one moment I did, somebody lost their life.

I feel terrible. No matter how I slice it. I'm responsible. If I hadn't let Trey leave that day, maybe this wouldn't have happened. Even if one of those other boys did this, they wouldn't have had the opportunity if I'd done my job and stayed at my post. And if it wasn't any of them, if I'd been in the detention room next to Moore's office, maybe I would've been able to catch the shooter. Or saved Moore's life.

But then again . . . maybe it's a blessing I wasn't there. Maybe I would've been shot too. Maybe Trey saved my life. I don't know.

No matter what, I can't shake it. Especially what I saw in Moore's office, under his desk. My heart dropped into my stomach. I don't know if anybody else even saw it. But as the ambulance wheeled Moore out, there on the floor sat Ramón's brush. How'd it get there if Ramón hadn't been in that room?

I didn't tell the cops because, well, I *don't* really know what happened, and the last thing I want to do is help them throw another brown boy behind bars, but damn. It's messing with me.

Could Ramón have done this? He's supposed to be one of the good ones.

Ms. Williamson

J.B.'s Mom

Dear Heavenly Father God,

I ask that you bless my baby boy. My only baby. I come to you humbly, Father God, and ask for forgiveness for any sins my beautiful son has committed, and ask that the truth be found. Truth that will prove his innocence.

Lord have mercy, Father God. J.B. is a good kid, a real good kid. He's not out there in them streets like other kids, he gets decent grades, and he don't get in no trouble. I know one of them other boys did that to Mr. Moore. Couldn't have been my J.B.

Please, God, please watch over my baby boy.

Amen.

J.B.'s Interrogation

(Transcript from J.B.'s Official Questioning)

DETECTIVE BO: State your name for the record, please.

J.B.: J.B.

DETECTIVE ASH: Whole name.

J.B.: Jabari Williamson.

DETECTIVE BO: Where do you live?

J.B.: Simple City.

DETECTIVE BO: So, you roll with Choppa Boyz?

J.B.: I don't.

DETECTIVE ASH: Where were you on the tenth of
October at approximately six thirty P.M.?

J.B.: . . .

DETECTIVE BO: You need to answer the question.

J.B.: School.

DETECTIVE BO: Where in school?

J.B.: Detention.

DETECTIVE BO: Why were you in detention? Are you a
troublemaker?

J.B.: NO!! I mean, no, I'm not. I didn't even
do anything. I wasn't supposed to be there.

It was my first time ever being up in
there.

DETECTIVE ASH: What did you hear?

J.B.: Not much. Just the shot.

DETECTIVE BO: And you didn't see anybody else go in
or out Moore's office?

J.B.: No.

DETECTIVE ASH: Did you like Principal Moore?

J.B.: . . .

DETECTIVE ASH: I SAID DI—

J.B.: I heard you!

DETECTIVE ASH: Then answer the question!

J.B.: I don't know, man.

DETECTIVE BO: So how do you feel about his death?
The Moore Method saved you, after all.

J.B.: Moore's method ain't do nothing for me.

DETECTIVE BO: Is that why you killed him?

J.B.: I'm done talking.

DETECTIVE ASH: Cut the crap, kid! Why were you
covered in Moore's blood if you have nothing to
do with this, huh?

DETECTIVE BO: And tell us about the altercation that
occurred between you and Moore earlier that day.

J.B.: Well—

DETECTIVE ASH: Do I have to remind you that it's not
looking good for you?! No more bullshit! No more
*I don't know*s, no more lies. The best hope you
have of helping your ass is to start talking.
Maybe the judge will see fit to take it easier on
you if you do . . .

ONE DAY BEFORE
THE MURDER

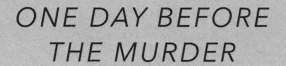

CHAPTER ONE

Simp

J.B.

I sit in class waiting for Mr. Finley to let us line up for dismissal. We're not supposed to move until the teacher holds up their index finger, but from the back of the class it's hard to see. There are four rows, with about eight kids in each, and because I'm tall, I'm always put in the last one.

I stare at the back of Brandon Jenkins's head. Peanut-shaped head. The worst. When he stands, I'll stand. Like usual.

I glance up at the wall above the SMART Board. The school's motto stares back at me: WE PROMISE.

Just thinking those two words makes the school anthem start playing in my head:

> *We promise.*
> *We are the young men of Urban Promise Prep.*
> *We are destined for greatness.*
> *We are college bound.*
> *We are primed for success.*
> *We are extraordinary because we work hard.*
> *We are respectful, dedicated, committed, and focused.*

We are our brother's keepers.
We are responsible for our futures.
We are the future.
We promise.

They made us memorize the thing when we got here in sixth grade. Three times a day and on command. More than the Pledge of Allegiance.

I look around at all the other boys, wondering if the anthem still plays in their heads too. All of us given the *promise* of a brighter future. Not like we needed that promise. Lots of us would probably go on to do big things with or without Principal Moore, but what do I know?

See, most boys land here because they struggled in regular school. The ones nobody wants to teach, the ones nobody understands. Principal Moore always talks about that being the reason he started the school, supposedly.

I guess it's worked for the most part.

I struggled all through elementary school. Not because I wasn't smart. But nobody cared enough to teach me in a way I could learn. At the time, I didn't even know there *were* different ways to learn.

So, when middle school came along, my mom put up a big fuss about how there were no public schools in our neighborhood she'd be comfortable sending me to. Then someone at my old school handed her a brochure for Promise, the best all-boys charter school in the city.

But from the very first day I never liked this place. The uniforms are stuffy. There's no "fraternizing" with other students. No talking at all unless it's to a teacher or adult. No music or cell phones. You can't even wear colored shoes or socks!

And you can't stand in class until the teacher holds up that index finger.

The recipe for making young men, Principal Moore always says.

Brandon stands so I do the same. The whole class jumps up at once like an army platoon. If we don't all stand in unison, most teachers will have us sit back down and try again, until we get it perfect. A tenet of the Moore Method: *Do all things neatly, completely, and perfectly with pride.*

If you want to get out of this place on time, you stand the right way on the first try.

Mr. Finley holds up two fingers. That means we can all face the door. After he flashes three fingers, we file in line with our hands behind our back.

"Dyson, that's one demerit for you," he calls out.

If your hands aren't locked in place behind your back, you get a demerit, in which case the teacher docks points from your "count."

Dyson shrugs and sucks his teeth.

"Make that two."

I shake my head. He should've known better.

Everybody's count starts at one hundred at the beginning of the day. If you earn a demerit, a teacher lowers your count on some dumb, noisy app on their tablet.

All the time, *beep . . . beep . . . beep* ringing throughout the halls. Worse than nails on a chalkboard. The messed-up part is there isn't a way to earn points back, you can only lose them. The shit is unfair.

Dyson gets one more. I shake my head. He's about to get detention for sure.

I walk behind Brandon, trying to focus on not messing up. Mr. Finley could've taken it easy on Dyson. He's usually no problem.

Seems like he's having a bad day. But I see things like that all the time at this school. Stuff I'm not sure any other kids or teachers see.

I guess I wouldn't know for sure though since I don't have many friends at school. Never hooped or played football, so I don't fit in with the athletes. Damn sure don't fit in with the nerds, the kids who love Promise. They rep this place like a gang or something. And I'm not really a trouble-maker anymore, so you won't catch me with the "hoodlums" as Principal Moore would say. The only teacher I can stand is Mrs. Hall because she takes it easy on us once the door to her classroom shuts. I don't have to worry so much about my count as long as we're getting down to work.

Just get through the day, I think to myself. Need to stick to my plan: Keep my head down, get these grades, and in exchange, go to college, far away from this place.

We file into the hallway, then everybody goes their separate ways and to their lockers.

"Let's go, young men, let's go!" Principal Moore shouts, doing his usual stroll. "Scholars don't waste time. Kings move with purpose—and that's what y'all are."

He's a big guy, to most. At 6'3", I'm a couple inches taller than him.

"Keep it moving! Let's have a great day full of promise, young men." His deep voice echoes through our hallways. He adjusts his tie. He's the type of guy that's buttoned up. Always. The perfect black luxury car that's always clean. The perfect leather briefcase with his initials embossed on the front. He even dresses perfectly. The knot in his tie, the shine on his belt buckle, the fold on the handkerchief in his front blazer pocket. The man's sharp. But he's rude as hell.

"Those shoes need shining, Malcolm. Go get the polish from Ms. Tate in my office."

"KeyShawn, too many wrinkles in those slacks. You know better. Grab the iron from Dean Hicks. Get yourself presentable."

"Time for a shape-up, Hugh. Looking a little rough. We can't have that. See me after school. I'll dust off my clippers."

Excellence. Another tenet of the Moore Method: *perfection, excellence, and discipline.* But at least he cares.

"Young man, are you missing your tie?" Principal Moore towers over one of the younger boys.

"Yes, sir," the boy says, looking down at his feet.

"Keep your head up."

The kid does as he's told, but avoids eye contact.

"Are you supposed to be in school without a tie?"

"No, sir."

"So, you made the choice to disrespect not only yourself but this school?"

"No, sir. I wasn't trying to disrespect nobody."

"Anybody," Principal Moore corrects.

"It won't happen again," he mutters.

"I know it won't, we'll see you in detention." Moore walks off.

We all look at each other, feeling sorry for the boy, but nobody's able to check on him because of the silent halls and stuff. I'm not about to lower my count.

I know that kid, though. Solomon. Not sure if Moore cared or not, but like a lot of families in this city, Solomon's family struggles. I don't know, maybe he only had one tie and something happened to it. But that's not an excuse to Moore, he couldn't care less. The wild part is Solomon's one of those kids that *likes* being at Promise.

But I don't have time to rescue anyone. I grab my things out of my locker, and keep it pushing.

I have to get out of here.

I burst through the school doors, my feet itching to step out of our perfect dismissal lines. But I wait until we hit the curb so we don't have to redo it all. The sun hits me and the familiar city noises surround us, a welcome soundtrack after a day of silence. There's literally no greater feeling than walking out of Promise Prep. The weight I've been carrying all day lifts. My shoulders broaden.

As the school building gets farther and farther out of sight, even my tongue relaxes and I feel like I can talk how I do around my way, back in Southeast. Promise is in Northeast. The area isn't great, but it ain't terrible either. Not like my hood, Benning Terrace.

I loosen my tie, wanting to get home and out of these uniform clothes. The navy-blue blazer and its matching straight-legged slacks that can't be too baggy or sag. The navy-blue button-up that *has* to be accompanied by the yellow-and-blue striped tie. Topped off by the black, hard-bottom dress shoes. Too much.

I head toward the bus, then get a text from my mom to go to the store to pick up chicken breasts and an onion. She probably knew I'd forget to let the chicken we already have in the freezer thaw.

I turn around and walk back toward Mariano's Grocery. I pass by a lot of guys I know. Everyone goes to Rocky's corner store after school, congregating and chopping it up. But I ignore them, walking straight past on the sidewalk. I don't have time to get mixed up with them.

During the ten-block walk, I try to empty my mind. For some reason, I can't stop thinking about Solomon. His eyes and the way he cowered when Moore got in his face. So I throw on my headphones and listen to a new beat I made, thinking of the perfect bars to drop on it. I need the distraction.

The grocery store is busy. I drift through with a basket, trying to quickly get what my mom needs. I cruise by the candy aisle, ready to grab a pack of Now and Laters, when I hear somebody saying my name. I snatch my headphones off.

"J.B., smile awhile! You'll feel better! You okay?" It's Mrs. Hall, and I'm surprised to see her, especially here. She's one of the original teachers, been at Promise since it first opened, and one of the only ones that's decent, but she still isn't a teacher you want to play with. Principal Moore doesn't even talk reckless to her. When she told us she'd be gone on maternity leave for a long time, everyone was bummed and confused. She didn't even look pregnant. But what do I know?

She makes her way over to me.

"Hey, Mrs. Hall, I'm fine. What are you doing?"

Her grocery cart spills over with healthy stuff, like I'd expect from somebody like her, but two cases of wine clink and clatter as she pushes her cart closer. Weird. Are you supposed to drink all that wine when having a baby? But my mom would say to mind my business.

"Same thing as you, it looks like." She smiles but her eyes seem filled with sadness, and she keeps biting her bottom lip.

"Yeah," I say. "Just getting some stuff for my mom."

"Everything alright at school?" she asks, her eyes growing more intense.

I shrug. "The usual, ma'am."

The usual bullshit, I want to say, but I keep it to myself, which my mom says is a bad habit.

She rocks left and right, a little off, distracted maybe.

"Are *you* okay?" I ask. "Were you visiting school?"

"Oh, I'm fine," she replies. "Just . . . missing teaching already. I always worry about you boys. I stopped by Promise for a meeting with Principal Moore. *That* went about as well as expected." There's anger tucked in her voice.

An awkward silence stretches between us. I start to respond, but she straightens her back as if she remembers where we are and who she's talking to, a student and not another adult. She says goodbye, then disappears around the corner into another aisle.

"That was weird," I whisper to myself.

I head to checkout. All the self-scans are closed so I have to deal with a cashier who makes a big show out of checking the twenty-dollar bill I pay with to make sure it's not counterfeit. I try to stay cool. It's fine. I'm used to it. But if this whole thing makes me miss the bus, I'm going to go off.

She finally lets me go and I hustle, barely making it aboard. I push my way through the rush hour crowd, hoping to find a seat though I know my chances are low.

I spot one all the way in the back, but as I make my way over I see it's next to Unk, the old man always roaming around the neighborhood. Not really in the mood to deal with him but luckily he's knocked out. Probably sleeping off a drink. If he was awake, he'd be running his mouth, either dropping some knowledge, spouting some profound outlook on life, or babbling about some wild conspiracy that seems so out there it just may be true.

I take out my phone, put in my headphones, and continue my music. I write some lines to the beat.

> Shawty I'm into you, not metaphorically though,
> the physical.

Pretty dope way to start a verse. Not like I'd ever rap it to the girl I'm thinking about while I'm writing. Keyana. She's, by far, the flyest girl in my neighborhood. She has this warm brown complexion and the smoothest skin I ever seen. Her hair falls down to her shoulders, each strand winding in its own unique way. Jet-black hair too, it doesn't turn brown in the sun or nothing.

Her eyes do though. When the light hits them just right, those brown eyes sparkle like her smile.

But more than all of that, Keyana wants the same thing I do: a chance to make it out of Benning Terrace and do something big. Something better than all the folks we see at home.

We've kicked it a few times, but she always has her guard up. Told me she doesn't really trust guys after some dickhead leaked some of their text messages. I can respect that. I told her I'd beat him up for her, but she wouldn't tell me who did it. But I know it was somebody at her school, Anacostia High.

I glance out the window. Keyana's school sits to the left. I crane to see if she's out front, hoping to get a glimpse of her but she's probably back around the way by now. We should be at that high school together.

But everybody (including my mom) thinks Promise is better and so perfect because of the college acceptance rate. Little do people know, Promise finds any reason to expel a kid once they realize the student has zero chance of getting into college. Kids are kicked out and thrown back into their neighborhood school their junior or senior year, with nobody to help them. And if they didn't have a chance at college before, they definitely don't have one once an expulsion goes on their record.

The bus screeches to a stop. I jump off and walk into the Benning Terrace complex. Simple City. Home. The gate creaks and I dodge water dripping from the ceiling. Some unknown leak gone unfixed. It's one of the oldest housing projects in DC and nobody cares about cleaning it up. The city keeps saying they're going to tear it down and rebuild, getting people all riled up. Black people, at least. The people who been here. The people who built this city. I wouldn't mind too much, though. Give us an excuse to move somewhere else.

I hustle through A block, moving through the square to where our apartment is.

As I approach, I catch Bando. He's a few years older than me. I think. With dudes like him you can never really tell. Every now and then I ask him to buy me a loosie or a brewski, so I guess he's around twenty-one because no one ever questions him. But he's also the type to have a fake ID, so no telling. Plus, no one messes with him. He's got reputation. We all know the hustlers who are about paper and only paper.

"J.B., what's good?" Bando daps me up, his hands super sweaty and hot.

"Not much, just getting home from school."

"True, slide with me right quick."

Bando never really gives you an opportunity to say no. He's so fast-talking I've watched him finesse his way out of a weed citation once. God level.

I follow him around the corner and into the alley behind our block. "Where we going, yo?"

"You 'bout to see." Bando steps between two big blue dumpsters and reaches into the designer pouch he wears. He stays fresh. "Check this."

He pulls out a handgun and holds it in his palm, completely non-chalant as if he's just showing me a collector's edition baseball card or something harmless like that. It's silver with a black handle. Small, but compact. My stomach drops at the sight of it. I've seen a gun before, but this feels really close. Too close. But I keep my face smooth—can't let anybody see me sweat.

I don't know much about guns, but I take a guess just to say something. "That a .38?"

"Hell yeah. Letting this joint go for a good price too. What you tryna' do?"

Panic rushes through me. I gulp and shake my head. "I'm good, son. That joint pretty, though." I don't mess with guns.

"Hell yeah, you know I'm 'bout quality. Shit, get at me if you change your mind. You know where I'll be, same place as always."

I do know. Kind of sad.

I leave the alley as Bando goes to take a piss.

Then as I head up the block, I spot her. Keyana. I freeze and sniff myself.

The thing I hate most about myself is the sweating. Every time I get nervous, embarrassed, self-conscious, anything, it never fails. My skin heats up and my armpits go into overdrive. My shirt's already halfway soaked from Bando showing me the gun, and now it's even worse.

I take a deep breath and try to keep my composure. I pop a stick of gum so my breath is right. "Calm down," I whisper to myself.

Keyana doesn't see me yet. "Look up, look up," I mutter under my breath. I want to see that big smile when she notices me. She'll roll her eyes, act annoyed how girls usually do, but I know deep down she wants to see me.

She starts to glance up, but a black BMW pulls up. The passenger window rolls down.

"What's good, slim?"

Keyana ignores the guy and keeps walking, but he follows, the car inching closer and closer. Her eyes dart all around and she finds me. But instead of a smile, her eyes say, *Help me.*

The dude in the BMW hops out. "Yo, you hear me?"

Laughter erupts from the car. There's someone else in there.

The dude grabs Keyana's arm, spinning her around, away from me.

"Yo, slow down. Why you running? You late or something? We can give you a ride. Where you want to go?"

"No, thank you, I'm okay," Keyana replies.

"You sure?"

"Yeah." She steps back.

"Well, at least let me get your number for my time." He licks his lips at her.

I run a little and interrupt them. "Keyana, you know him?"

They both look my way. Up close, the dude seems a little older, maybe eighteen. I still tower over him. He looks me up and down and flinches.

Even though I used to be scared to fight, I use my size to intimidate people all the time. I never had to *actually* fight until I got to middle school. I won so many to the point where I didn't mind them so much. I mean, I wasn't ever going to start one, but I sure didn't mind finishing the job.

"Who you?" the dude asks.

"I'm her boyfriend, who you?"

Of course, I'm not really her boyfriend, though I'd like to be. But some of my homegirls always make me pretend to be their boyfriend when dudes try to talk to them. In reality, though, nobody's falling for that, we all know that game.

The dude takes a step toward me. "Who you talking to?"

As we close in on each other, Keyana steps up to stop us. She looks at me. "It's okay, babe, let's just go."

We walk away.

The dude follows us, shouting, "Man, don't nobody want your ugly ass anyway!"

Keyana squeezes my hand, trying to hold me in place because she can probably feel my desire to turn around.

"Simp ass," he says.

I snap.

I spin.

"What you say?"

"You heard me, simp." He scowls at me.

There's a lot of ways I could handle this moment, but maybe it's because Keyana is standing here with me? Maybe it's because I had a long day at school? Maybe it's because I hate being disrespected? Maybe a combination of all three.

But, I swing.

I catch the dude with a hard right and he folds. His boy rushes out the car to pick him up off the ground. He clearly doesn't want any problems with me.

Keyana tugs at my hand. I'm afraid to turn around and look at her because I know how disappointed she's gonna be.

I blew it. I should've kept my cool.

She gives me a final yank. "J.B., let's go!"

I look in her eyes, ready for her to be angry with me. But her eyes fill with happiness, even a giddy excitement.

"Come on, let's get out of here!" She's almost laughing.

By now a small crowd has gathered. Onlookers videotape the guy who got knocked out as his boy drags him to the car.

Keyana and I head in the opposite direction. Our walk turns into a skip, a skip into a light jog, and I start to sweat again when I realize where we're headed.

Her house.

CHAPTER TWO

Boyfriend

J.B.

We sit on Keyana's bed as she holds a pack of ice to my right hand. Old boy's tooth got me. I try to ignore the pain, though. I've never been in Keyana's house, let alone in her bedroom, but her space looks exactly how I always pictured it: magazine clippings, vintage hip-hop posters, and album covers line her walls. Everything's neat, and the room smells so good.

As she's working on my hand, I study her face, the curve of her lips, and how long her eyelashes are, and the tiny freckles she has on her nose. I want to kiss her. I want to know what her mouth tastes like. I want to be close to her. I try to look away but I'm locked in.

Keyana interrupts my daydream. "You okay?"

"Huh? Yeah, I'm good. You?"

"Uh-huh." She laughs. "You didn't have to do all that, you know? Back there."

"He shouldn't have treated you like that. He was reckless with his mouth."

"I mean, you're right, he definitely deserved that."

The sun sets. Golden light creeps through her window, hitting her brown eyes. Sexy as hell. I want to wrap my arms around her and press her soft skin to mine. I want her to feel how hard my heart beats when I'm near her. I want her to know how I feel about her.

"Soooo, did you mean what you said?" she asks.

"About what?"

Her eyebrow lifts. "About being my boyfriend. You were pretty convincing."

"How could I mean that? You know you ain't my girl."

"That's 'cause you're in the streets. Probably got all types of girls you're talking to."

I smile and shake my head. "Nah, not at all."

Everyone keeps calling me a player. Not sure how or why, I've only been with one girl. There are guys on my block who talk about being with women 24/7. That's not me. Not because I can't. Girls are into me, I know that . . . but I'm rarely interested back. Until Keyana.

I need something more than just a pretty face. I need someone who makes me want to be a better person. Keyana does that for me. She's smart, talented, and can be funny as hell. I admire her, and that's hard to come by.

But every time we get close, she pulls back, claiming I'm not really serious or that I have other girls. That can't be further from the truth. I need to prove that to her.

"Even if I was, I'd be willing to change for you." I lick my lips like I've seen older guys on the block do. Which is probably dumb. I don't know if I look cool, or downright goofy. *Stay calm. Be cool*, I think. If the nerves hit, so does the sweat.

"Yeah right." Keyana puts away her makeshift first aid kit.

If there was ever going to be a chance to make a move, this is it. I'm sitting on her bed and it's just the two of us. But still, a little voice inside me doesn't want to move too fast. I need to know she wants me as badly as I want her.

I need the moment to be perfect.

"I got something for you." I take out my phone, trying to will my hands to stop shaking.

"Oh yeah, what's that?"

I figure there's only one thing that will show Keyana how serious I am about her. The one thing I've never shared with anyone. My rhymes.

I clear my voice and begin to read what I wrote earlier . . .

". . . Shawty I'm into you, not metaphorically though, the physical,

Scared to tell you I'm digging you, don't know if it's reciprocal,

These feelings nonsensical, I can't escape it

I love your beautiful tone, you perfectly shaded,

Let me serenade you, with—

Sweet soliloquies solidified by googly eyes,

Google couldn't find the love I can provide,

It's something Wikipedia couldn't describe and dictionary dot com couldn't define,

I'm just hoping you'd be mine."

Silence stretches between us after I finish. I'm frozen, unable to move my phone from in front of my face. I don't want to make eye contact. A bead of sweat skates down my back.

Maybe she hates it?

Finally, I get the courage to look at her and spot Keyana attempting to hide a smile. "Damn, you couldn't memorize that shit, boy?"

We both fall out laughing.

"Well, you like it?" I ask.

"Yeah. You did your thing or whatever." She flashes me a shy smile.

"I wrote it for you."

"Yeah?" She looks down, innocently, almost sad. I don't know why, but something tells me to pull her close, so I grab her hand and gently move her closer to me.

"Your peoples home?" I ask.

"Nope, probably won't be for a little bit. Why?"

"Just asking." I take a deep breath.

Keyana looks at me with a sly smile. I think she knows what's on my mind.

She inches even closer to me at the edge of the bed. My hands move to her hips, hers to my chest. Our eyes only lock for a split second before our lips become magnets.

When we kiss, electricity shoots through my skin. I try to sink into the feeling. I'm kissing the girl I like. It's really happening.

Keyana pulls back.

My eyes snap open. "You okay?"

"Yeah, I'm good. I'm sorry."

"No need to apologize, just tell me what I did wrong." I take her hand in mine.

Keyana hesitates, nibbling her bottom lip. She opens and closes her mouth several times before the words finally make their way out. "It's not what you did, it's what you gonna do."

"What do you mean?! What am I going to do?" My mind races. What is she worried about? Can't she tell how I feel about her?

She looks up into my eyes. "I really like you, J.B. Like more than I've liked anybody, and I've been crushing on you for a while, I'll admit."

I start cheesing and I can't even hide my smile.

She rests her head on my shoulder. "And I'm so afraid to, like, go there with us, and see that you don't like me like that."

It's wild seeing her so vulnerable. The most beautiful girl in the world, worried about *me* liking *her*.

"Keyana, do you know I think about you all the time? I've never liked a girl this much. That's because you're different, and I see that. You gotta see that I'm different too."

She sits upright. Her eyes hold surprise and she purses her lips. I can tell she's thinking. I can tell she's considering.

I hug her. "I'll never do anything to hurt you, Keyana. I'll only protect you."

She gazes up to me. "You promise?"

"I promise," I assure her.

She kisses me again.

"You ready to be my girl?" I ask.

She blushes. "Yeah."

"Like for real?"

"Yeah, for real."

The moment happens so quick and easy, I don't even know how to process it.

I just did it. I just made Keyana Glenn my girlfriend.

She kisses me again, pushing me back onto the bed and I pull her down with me.

For a brief second, all my worries are forgotten. I don't care about Promise Prep. I don't care about getting into college. I don't even care about making it out of Benning Terrace. All I care about is the girl in front of me, thankful that she trusts me enough to share herself.

When it's over we just look at each other until we both start giggling.

"What's funny?" she asks.

"Nothing, you're just cute." I kiss her forehead.

"You think so?"

"I know so."

She smiles. "You're cute too."

She comes in for a kiss when, *Wumpth*. Keyana's front door closes downstairs. Panic fills her eyes. "I think that's my mom." She hops up like a damn karate kid and jets to her bedroom window. "J.B., come on! You gotta go!"

"You want me to jump out a window?!" I snatch up my clothes, trying to pull them on at lightning speed.

"Boy, you tall as shit, you ain't gon' fall that much!" she says, shoving me forward.

I laugh while rushing to the window, but I turn back and give Keyana one last kiss.

"I'll call you tonight," she says.

I tumble down.

Keyana was wrong about the fall, but it was worth it.

I get home just before dark. Soon as I open the door, the mouthwatering smell of baked chicken hits me. My mom's baked chicken. I guess the chicken that was in our freezer did thaw in time. She only cooks them when either something really good happened or something really bad. Anxiety floods through me as I walk down the hall. I hope she's not crying over the stove. I hope it's something good, something to celebrate.

"Ma?"

"In the kitchen!" she shouts back.

I head to the kitchen and can barely see her under the steam rising from the stove. She's humming one of her church tunes. A good sign. She doesn't hum when really bad things happen.

"What's up, Ma?"

"Why are you home so late?" She squints her eyes, scanning me like she's looking for the lie.

"Mannnnn, the bus broke down. Had to walk." I look away, attempting to hide the truth.

"Uh-huh, you get those items from the store?"

I take the groceries out of my bag and throw them in the fridge. I pray the chicken hasn't gone bad since I made a detour.

"How was school?" she asks.

"It was school."

She gazes back into her pot. "Well, get cleaned up, dinner will be ready soon."

"Okay, how *you* feeling?"

My mom glances up at me with hopeful eyes. "I'm feeling okay, baby."

I nod. Sometimes the really good thing that happens is not having the really bad thing come. Seems like one of those days.

I go to my room and start to daydream about Keyana. I wonder if she likes baked chicken. I want to learn to cook as good as my mom for the both of us.

I don't want Keyana to have a life like my mom. She deserves better. That's why I work so hard in school, so I'll be able to take care of my mom and my future wife.

I look up at the crack still in my ceiling. The one the landlord doesn't care about. He keeps ignoring my mom's calls about fixing it. I can't wait to have the money to move her out of this place.

I start to text Keyana but stop myself. I don't want to seem too pressed. I want to wait for her to text me first, but what if she feels the same way so she doesn't text me either?

My hands get all itchy. Ugh. If I wait too long maybe she'll think

I'm not thinking about her. Why does this have to be so hard? Is this what love is? Am I in love? I have to be, right?

I text her.

> **J.B.:** Your ma know I was there?

> **Keyana:** Nope we're good.

> **J.B.:** When you gonna call me?

> **Keyana:** At 8 when I'm done with homework.

I smile. That's Keyana, focused. I love it. I get cleaned up and head to the dining room. I've worked up an appetite.

I barely even taste my mom's chicken as I scarf it down, my eyes glued on my phone, waiting until it flashes 8:00 P.M.

When it rings, I dart from the table.

"Boy, if you don't . . ."

I can't even hear my mom scolding me. I'm already in my room and picking up before the third ring.

"Hey . . ." I try to make my voice sound smooth and not out of breath from running to my room.

"Hey," she replies. Her phone voice is so nice. I could listen to her for hours.

I lie on the bed and start asking her a bunch of questions. We talk about how it's fate I saw her walking down my block, leaving her homegirl's house that day. She calls me ridiculous for knocking old boy out, and I like it. It makes me feel like I can protect my girl. We talk about how good we make each other feel. We talk about our future and how we're going to make it out of Benning Terrace and live in Hollywood one day. I'll be some big-time rapper and Keyana will be a lawyer. We'll be a power couple.

"J.B., don't play me, I swear to God," she says.

"You don't have to worry, Key." I try to make sure she hears how serious my voice is.

"So now that we official, when you taking me out?"

"How about tomorrow? There's a playoff game at Promise. I'll meet you at Anacostia and we can go over together."

Basketball games are the perfect place to stunt 'cause kids from all over the city will be there, all dressed to impress, trying to look cool. But nothing is cooler than having a bad girl on your arm. Everyone will be jealous that Keyana's my girl now.

"You promise?" she asks.

"I'll always keep my word. I got you."

"I believe you," she says.

Music to my ears. I want to be that different kind of guy. The one who always shows up. The one who's loyal. The one who's hers.

"You snore?" I ask her.

"What?" She sucks her teeth like she's mad.

"Do you snore when you sleep?"

"Noooo. Why?"

"'Cause we gonna talk all night. I got mad questions, and I don't want you snoring in my ear."

"Whatever. Bet you snore like a champ. Bet you could win a whole-ass snoring competition."

We laugh until I get the hiccups.

Keyana and I stay up the rest of the night talking on the phone, falling asleep, listening to each other breathe. Anything to feel close.

THE DAY OF THE MURDER

J.B.

CHAPTER THREE

Strap

J.B.

At school the next day, I'm no good. I can't focus on anything the teachers say. I'm in a bubble where all I hear is Keyana's laugh. My eyes glaze over and I start daydreaming about her lips on mine. The soft feel of her skin. The way her neck smells when I'm kissing it.

It's Mrs. Hall's class, American History, but Mr. Finley's subbing now that she's on maternity leave. Truth is, even though Promise is one of the best schools in the city, teachers never stay more than two years. Feels like they're here one moment and gone the next. I'm not sure if it's because of us or because of Principal Moore. I've seen the way he talks to them—he's harder on them than we are.

Mr. Finley drones on and I wish we were doing one of Mrs. Hall's wacky interactive learning games to get us to memorize the World War II facts. I think about seeing her yesterday, the multiple bottles of wine in her cart, eyes all sad. I hope she's doing okay.

"Take out your independent reading book. If you don't have one, I've got a few up here. I don't want to see anything but y'all reading! Eyes on the page!" Mr. Finley shouts like the classroom isn't completely silent and we can't hear him.

I need a break. I hold up three fingers—code for *bathroom*—and pretend to read *The Autobiography of Malcolm X* while I wait for Mr. Finley to let me go. I bite my bottom lip, ready for him to say no because of how frequent bathroom trips "disrupt instructional time." The teacher version of an asshole.

But surprisingly, Mr. Finley glances up from his sudoku puzzle and nods, giving me permission to leave.

I hit the hallway and check the line. The blue strip snaking along both sides of the hallway. I focus on staying directly on it so a school resource officer or a passing teacher won't say anything to me. *The blue path keeps you out of the red zone*, Principal Moore always says, reminding us that it's supposed to help us become the best version of a young man we can be—no ruckus and no fighting. Which it does, I guess.

I round a corner. Beeps flood the hall, bouncing off cold, gray walls, and slipping beneath classroom doors. The long walk to the bathroom always reminds me of visiting my dad over in the DC jail. His sad uniform, the noise of the sliding metal doors, the barking guards, the lines of prisoners. I never want to be like him.

I make a left and prepare to head to the basement bathrooms. Less traffic down there and way cleaner.

A voice stops me.

"I'm not going to tell you again!"

I look around. At first I think they're talking to me, but I don't see anyone.

"I'm being very fair in my expectations . . . !"

I know that voice—Dean Hicks. Principal Moore's enforcer.

"Don't you walk away from me when I'm talking to you!"

I can't figure out who he's talking to. But I don't have time to catch the dean's wrath today. That white man loves ruining people's days. Never seems to acknowledge he's not like *us*. Like some of the other teachers, you can tell they know they're white, talking to us in a weird, high-pitched voice, trying to make friendly banter. Trying to *identify* or seem "down." But it really just sounds like the way you talk to animals at the zoo.

"Good riddance!" Dean Hicks barks.

I crane to listen even harder. My curiosity getting the best of me. Right now it sounds like he wants to beat this student's ass.

I realize too late that his voice is closer than it was before. Dean Hicks sweeps around the corner, nearly running right into me.

"What are you doing in the hallway, Williamson?" he says, agitation turning his voice into a growl.

He's all red and sweaty, and I wonder which boy has taken him to the edge like this. Somebody must have really stepped out of line for him to be this fired up.

"Did you hear me?" he repeats.

"Bathroom, sir."

"Then why are you standing around here?" he shouts. "Get moving."

I just nod and answer, "Yes, sir," because I learned early on using "sir" and "ma'am," and these teachers pretty much leave you alone.

I walk fast down those stairs. The heat of his gaze burns my back. I roll my eyes. My theory's always been guys like Dean Hicks, Principal Moore, Mr. Reggie, were cornballs when they were my age. So now, they need to feel powerful, taking their issues out on us. It's messed up, but I don't care.

I hit the last stall and do my business.

I wish I had my phone to text Keyana. I hate the no cell phones rule even more right now.

I go to flush, but it won't work. The handle won't even catch. I search the back of the toilet, trying to fix it. There's nothing worse than somebody who doesn't flush. The lid's shifted off just a little.

I lift it up, attempting to reposition it, and freeze.

I see a gun.

A big strap, much bigger than the gun Bando showed me yesterday. It's black with ridges on the top. Looks like a damn military piece. Special issue, black ops, some shit you'd have on a video game or see in the movies. My whole body goes numb.

Was this a trap? How'd it even get here? Who brought it? Sweat pours down my face. *Why would someone bring a gun to our school? What the hell?! What am I going to do?*

I can't go to the teachers. If word gets out I snitched about something this bad, there could be serious repercussions. But I can't leave it here 'cause if someone *is* thinking of using it, there could still be serious issues.

Shit, shit, shit. I pace back and forth. I have to get the hell away from this. I ignore the beads of sweat dripping down my forehead, my clammy palms, and my heartbeat going wild. I wash my hands and leave. With each step I take, my feet feel like they're bricks. I gulp. *Just keep going,* I think. Get as far away from here as possible.

Back in the hall, I pass by a short Latino kid. I forget his name, but he nods at me. I nod back. He holds up a bag.

"¡Mirá! Let me know if you're hungry. I got pupusas," he says.

I shake my head. I can't even think about food right now. I can't even speak. I might just throw up. He gives me a thumbs-up before he turns away.

After he gets farther down the hall, I remember him. The kid who's always trying to sell something. Sometimes food, sometimes drinks, candy. He used to post up outside of Rocky's, but the owner wasn't having it and told him not to come back. He reminds me of Bando. Trying to make a buck.

I hold my breath and glance over my shoulder to see if he goes in the bathroom. I watch him disappear inside. He doesn't strike me as the type to bring a pistol to school. But then again, I don't know him very well.

I need to take my mind off that gun. I try to think about all the things I'm going to say to Keyana when I meet her for the game after school. Maybe we go back to her house afterward and hang out.

I get a demerit for not paying attention in calc and mess up my count, but I don't even care right now. I have to stay focused on something, anything but that gun in the bathroom.

Mr. Kim lets us go a few minutes early and I'm out of there in a flash.

The halls aren't silent the way they usually are, but today that's not our fault. The Promise students walk the line and pack up, but there are other people buzzing around. The important folks that have Principal Moore beaming and shaking hands and being overly nice to us. Donors like Mr. Ennis walking around and taking pictures. Or community volunteers painting banners and hanging them up. This is when you see the most white people at school.

I dodge a white girl who doesn't know the blue line is for us. She passes me, stone-faced and rude, but I don't care. Dean Hicks leads them all down another corridor and out of sight.

As I pack up, sweat drips down my face. I squeeze my eyes shut and no matter what I do, the image of that gun pops back in like its taunting me to take it, to get rid of it *permanently* before it ends up doing what guns do . . . kill people.

A voice inside me whispers: *Why is this my responsibility?* I think about what my mom would say. If I get caught with it, I'd risk ruining everything. No one would believe it wasn't mine and it'd go on my record. Hell, I might end up in juvie.

I check my phone to distract me from making a bad decision—just as I thought, it's full of texts from Keyana. I smile reading the franticness of them.

> **Keyana:** hey u, still meeting me, right?

> **Keyana:** J.B. ???

> **Keyana:** really?????

> **Keyana:** J.B., I swear to god u better not be ignoring me . . . 4 your own sake.

It's kind of cute. I start to text her back, to let her know I didn't have my phone and to confirm our date for later. I don't want her stressed. I don't want her to ever worry.

Before I can press SEND, the phone flies out of my hand.

What the—?

I look up. Principal Moore glares back at me. The vein in his dark forehead bulges. His eyes look sunken and his clothes disheveled, the top button on his shirt undone.

"*NO* phones during school hours. You know that!" he yells, sweat coating his forehead.

"Are you for real? School is over!" I say.

The school bell rings. Moore holds his finger up. "*Now* school is ended. Phone is mine. Detention is yours."

He can't be serious. This was petty even for Principal Moore.

Panic floods me. I *can't* get detention. Not today. And even if I did,

I *have* to tell Keyana what's going on. The last thing I need is her thinking I'm blowing her off. The last thing I want to do is stand her up.

"Yo, this is bullshit, you can't be serious. I'm literally packing up to leave school." The words all run together. I'm so mad. "Mr. Kim let us out early. This isn't fair."

Principal Moore gets in my face. So close I can smell his breath. The scents of acid and . . . liquor hit me. "You watch who you talking to, you little shit. You understand me? You are a child, you curse at me again and I'mma put you in a child's place." He talks in a low tone, almost a whisper.

I'm stunned into silence. Anger bubbles up in me. I ball my fists. Everyone in the hallway freezes. Who does he think he is, taking my phone? My personal property? I follow all his rules. I do whatever the teachers—and he—ask for.

"Did you hear me?" Principal Moore yells.

I black out. My heart backflips. I spit in Moore's face.

Moore grabs me by the collar, shoving me into a locker. My head clobbers the metal. I'm pinned in place.

"I will break you," he barks, and now his spit's all over my face.

Classroom doors fling open. Moore drops me and I fall like a damn doll.

Kids flood the hallways passing us every which way, oblivious to this lunatic. Teachers poke their heads out of their classrooms to watch.

"I'll see you in detention. Meanwhile, I'll be getting those expulsion papers ready." His eyes burn into mine.

My heart sinks. I think of my mom. I think of him calling her about this. I open my mouth to start to apologize. If I get expelled from this school it'll crush her. How will I get out of this city and into college with an expulsion on my record?

My heart pounds ten times harder like it's trying to escape. Rage builds up in me.

BAM! I slam my fist into the cold, gray locker. The metal bends under the pressure. The warped slivers slice through my knuckles and warm blood trickles down my hand.

Younger kids pass by, staring at me like they're watching the aftermath of a car wreck.

"No worries. Your mom will be paying for that," Principal Moore threatens, his voice a scary calm. He strides off.

My skin boils. My mind floods with all the possible ways I could hurt Moore. All I'd have to do was follow him to his office, lock the door behind me and go to work, beat his ass one good time. I think I could take him.

"I'mma see you," I mumble to myself and think of that gun in the basement.

I'mma see him for sure.

PART TWO

Trey

THE WASHINGTON POST
THE MOORE METHOD
SAVES LIVES

Charter schools. Magnet schools. Federal takeovers. At one time or another, all have been suggested as the solution to turn around the generally dismal performance of DC Public Schools.

The challenges that face urban schools–from outdated resources, to overcrowded buildings, to widespread teacher burnout–are numerous and daunting, but most have their roots in a single recalcitrant reality.

"The two-ton elephant in every urban classroom is poverty," says Wilson Hicks, dean of the student body at Urban Promise Prep, a school that may have finally solved the problem of educational inequity.

Hicks adds, "Students lack discipline, not capacity to learn. Underprivileged kids are less likely to come to school with an appreciation for what education can bring. When you're living in an area where you're surviving day-to-day, seeing education as something to work at is hard. That's why the Moore Method works. We are all about discipline."

Hicks notes that former principal Kenneth Moore preached excellence to his students. His philosophy revolved around teaching kids to be their best selves despite the challenges life may throw at them. And it seems to have worked: Urban

Promise Prep had the highest standardized test scores of any public school in DC, for the third year in a row.

Sadly, Moore was recently shot to death at Urban Promise Prep. Though there have been no official arrests in the murder, police are investigating three suspects.

Present Day

Solomon Bekele

Urban Promise Prep Student

Yeah, I know who did it. Know why too.

Everybody thinks it was J.B., but it wasn't. He was one of the few students I actually liked. Sure, he didn't talk much, but at least he didn't pick on me in third period like the rest of the kids.

Couldn't have been Ramón either. Committing a murder on school grounds? Nah, I'm in math with him, he's way too smart for that. He has big dreams he wouldn't risk by doing something stupid and getting locked up for life. No, it was the other one. The one who doesn't care about anything.

Trey.

I never liked him. I didn't have any classes with him, but I'd see him at lunch and recess all the time. He always had something to say about my Ethiopian accent, my complexion, and the scent of my clothes. He teased me about my clothes in general. And we wear uniforms! That takes some next-level assholery!

I hated him, actually. Glad I never stood up to him, though, because it turns out he's a murderer. And he didn't kill just anybody. He killed Principal Moore.

Takes some balls. In some ways I admire him because of that. His willingness to stand up for himself. That's exactly what he did a few hours before the murder, when Moore first gave him detention.

A lot of kids knock Moore, but I don't. My parents taught me respect, and if you respect Moore, you'll get along just fine. It's *literally* his job to boss us around; he's the principal and the founder.

J.B. knew respect. Ramón knew respect. But Trey—Trey didn't respect anyone. My parents would KILL me if I even thought of talking back.

I guess Trey was raised differently.

I guess he was raised to kill.

Stanley Ennis

Entrepreneur and Urban Promise Prep Donor

Nobody understood Moore's vision like I did. In fact, I think I saw more potential in what he built than even he did. Promise is more than just a school . . . it's a movement, and more importantly, a legacy.

Not everyone saw it that way, though. People are often too small-minded or outright jealous to have the vision. There were always people complaining about the way Moore did things: staff, students, parents, even community members.

Of course, Moore wouldn't let that stop him. We spoke about expanding Promise, creating a network of schools across the country that would do exactly what Promise did in DC. Get the results that brought in the big bucks. Takes gumption and know-how. Moore had the know-how, and I definitely had the gumption.

Moore wanted to grow slow at first. But after that first check I wrote to the school, he started to see things my way.

Expanding the vision started with the basketball team. A strong sports department can be leveraged nationally. So, it's a real shame that kid Trey played for the team. This year felt charmed. We were primed to go all the way to the championships, having our boys' photos splashed across every newspaper and national news. Opening up the wallets of the wealthier donors we needed to take Promise to the next level.

I didn't mind giving the kids as much money as they needed with a team showing out like that. Moore was even able to start a new initiative for the kids, the Promise Fund. It had a nice tagline: "To fund our students' biggest dreams and cement their futures." As much money as I poured into that investment, I told him he should've named it the Ennis Promise Fund!

Again, such a shame he's gone. We were on the verge of accomplishing something incredible, and maybe we still can. I wonder who will step in to manage all this. With a tragedy of this magnitude, I'm positive I can usher in substantial financial support. Maybe we'll rename the Promise Fund after all.

Brandon Jenkins

Urban Promise Prep Student

Trey is my best friend here. I play the one, he plays the two.

Our basketball team wasn't all that good before, but then Trey transferred in from New York. As soon as he got here, it went up. We got good.

By the end of our junior year, Trey was the top scorer on the team. Shit, he even upped my game. Not only were we having our best season ever, but we got real looks from colleges in the area. That's all I've ever dreamed of—playing college ball.

The day of the shooting was a playoff game against Dunbar, another powerhouse school in the city. The news kept saying that so many college scouts would be there. Trey and I had been studying Dunbar's best players and we had a pretty solid plan to take them down. I felt good about it.

Until I saw Trey that morning.

I knew something was up when he wasn't smiling. He smiled every day, especially on game days.

"You good, Slime?" I asked.

"I'm straight," he replied quietly.

When I say "Slime," he says "Goon." It's our thing. Always. But not today.

He walked off fast, but I called out after him:

"Trey, what's going on?

"Trey, talk to me.

"Trey, you bugging."

He finally stopped. It took him like thirty long seconds to turn around and face me. He stared back with weird, bloodshot eyes, then led me into a nearby bathroom.

I followed.

"You have to PROMISE you won't tell anybody," he said.

I promised.

Trey closed his eyes, took a deep breath, and right when he went to open his mouth to speak, a morning rush of kids came bursting in. Trey just looked at them, looked at me, and stormed out.

I don't know what he was going to tell me in that moment, but I went to class with a funny feeling in my stomach, like . . . like something bad might happen.

I didn't see Trey again until warm-ups before the game. He crept into the gym looking even more pitiful than he had that morning.

"Gather around," Coach Robinson shouted. "Trey has an announcement." Coach gritted his teeth and I knew whatever Trey was about to say would be bad.

"I can't play," Trey mumbled.

"Speak up, young man," Coach said. "Own your mistake and this consequence."

"I got in trouble." He muttered an explanation.

Apparently Principal Moore gave Trey detention and he couldn't play in the game tonight. The whole team erupted. Disappointed moans and groans, dudes sucking they teeth, some dropping their heads in defeat. A chorus of *"Damn, Trey"* echoed through the gym.

But I stayed silent.

I couldn't even look up at him. I just gawked at my shoes. I could feel him staring at me, waiting for me to say, "It's all good," or to tell the team, "We still got this, y'all," but I couldn't. I never met his eyes.

The next time I saw Trey, handcuffs circled his wrists and officers marched him out of the school.

I don't want to believe Trey killed Principal Moore. I know the *real* him. I know a side of Trey that nobody else gets to see, and I owe it to him to give him the benefit of the doubt. But then, I think about how bugged out he was that morning. It's not looking good for him.

Uncle T

Trey's Uncle

I really hope Trey ain't take my gun. For my sake and *his*. I mean, Trey's a lot of things, but he isn't dumb. And he isn't a killer. I know 'cause I am.

I served over twenty years for this country in the marines, Special Ops. Three tours. Lived a lot, learned a lot. And the evil I've seen don't exist in Trey.

However, when I first picked my nephew up from New York, he had knucklehead written all over him. Same as me at his age, only I behaved far worse. Stayed in the streets heavy and had either death, prison, or the military as my options. The war saved me, if I'm honest. Which is a weird thing to think about. Being shipped abroad to go fight for a country who doesn't love you, kill strangers as the only option to keep you alive. Trey don't got the heart for war, though, I know that much.

But I owed it to my sister to take Trey in and make sure he had a better fate than the guys I grew up with. What I didn't expect was for Trey's attitude to be as bad as it was. Always talking back, always bucking the rules, the type of thing that Black men can't afford to do. It's probably because his father died so young. Cancer took him and left

Trey behind to be raised by a woman. So, I made it my mission to get him right. Whatever it took.

Curfews, strict routines, trying to keep him either in school or at home, limiting his time in the world, giving him zero space to get into trouble. There's a lot of mess you can get into in this city.

Sure, every now and then, we bump heads, especially at first. The transition is a hard thing for anyone. And Trey didn't make it easy, trying my patience time and again. Coming in late, being unappreciative, neglecting his chores. I told him there was an easy way to do things, and there was a hard way all the same. He chose the hard way each and every time, and eventually I had to chin-check the boy to get him to straighten out.

It's not like I wanted to, but I didn't really know what else to do. Ain't like I ever raised a boy into a young man before. I know how I came up, and I ended up doing alright for myself. Better than most.

After seeing these hands were the only thing that worked, I proceeded to pop him every now and again so he knew I wasn't playing. Eventually, we got into a rhythm and he started following the rules at home, but then the trouble at school came.

For some reason, those people down at Promise always seemed to have a problem with Trey. They made me sit in class with him a couple times. Of course, he behaved like an angel *then*.

I got on him about things and I thought we'd turned a corner. I hadn't heard from the school for a good few weeks. I was beginning to think I really did it, I really set my nephew on a new path.

I'll be honest: I care for the boy, I really do. I know he thinks I just want to ride him, but he doesn't understand that this world will swallow him whole if his head isn't on straight. Black men don't get second chances, yet Trey got one with me. I couldn't let him waste it.

And I got to give credit where it's due, he's been trying lately. I'm proud of him for the strides he made in basketball. I went to a few of his games and the kid impressed me. I even invited one of my guys from the navy to his playoff game. Bragged on Trey. Told him my nephew was the star player and a good kid. They sat in the bleachers waiting to meet the famous Trey Jackson, the next NBA star. But of course, Trey never played in that game. His own fault. Embarrassed the hell out of me.

I know Trey didn't do anything to Principal Moore, but I can't ignore the fact my pistol is missing. Why couldn't Trey just do the right thing? If he never had detention he would've been playing in that game and his innocence wouldn't be a question. This is exactly the thing I tried to explain to that boy. As a Black man, you get no benefit of the doubt. You have to be on the right side of everything.

My head is a mess though. Thoughts on a loop about what I could've done differently. I tried so hard to change him, to turn him around, and he still found himself caught up in this messed-up system. This place is too hard for a Black man.

I don't know, maybe I was too hard on him too.

Coach Robinson

Urban Promise Prep Basketball Coach

'm not going to lie, this one got me good. On both sides of the ball. Principal Moore gave me a shot when others didn't. I coached rec ball before this job. All for the love of the game because it wasn't putting any money in my pocket.

Moore and I go way back. We attended Hampton University together. I got into some trouble off campus, and got kicked off the team. It screwed up my chances at going to the league. Coaching was the next best thing. It keeps me close to the game.

When Moore decided to start a team at Urban Promise, I was the first person he called. That's Moore. Always looking out. Always making sure everybody around him could eat. Even some of these players.

Moore said the better the team did, the more potential for sponsorship dollars. He had me and the coaching staff scout players from here to New York, and he reached out personally to invite kids to Promise. He even would give them cash if they needed it to help them get here. That man helped so many families.

After a few years, we started actually competing instead of losing every game. Then we got this kid, Brandon, and things really started shaping up.

And then came Trey.

That boy reminds me so much of myself, but with more talent. That's the sad part. Too many kids with so much potential fall to the pressure of the system. An invisible weight that pins them all down. They can't even see it.

But the thing is, Trey didn't do this. Trey wouldn't hurt a fly. Trey is one of the sweetest kids I know. Here's an example: One time Moore got all riled up, giving a kid a hard time—not one of my players. A quiet kid. I think Omar? Omari? Well, he wasn't wearing a belt and was going to get written up. Guess what happened? Trey walked over and gave the kid his belt. He was wearing his basketball uniform, so Moore couldn't write him up, and he covered for that kid, just like that. That's Trey. That's how he is.

Still, even if he's innocent, I think this'll ruin him. I think it'll traumatize him, and I think that's the flaw of the system. Once it touches you, you tainted forever, guilty or not. Same thing happened to me.

Now Moore's gone. Trey's gone.

I don't know, man, I'm just messed up.

Antoine Betts

Urban Promise Prep Student

saw the whole thing, uh-huh. The whole thing.

Trey came in with the first lunch period, lunch Block A. They say Block A is the rowdy kids but that's my favorite one. Them boys funny as hell—I stay laughing.

I was there because I'm doing SCI—Senior Culinary Initiative— and getting credit for cooking so I can have the option to work in a restaurant after high school, who knows.

Apparently, SCI was an idea this dude Ramón created. The lunch ladies love it because they're understaffed and when me and the other SCI dudes have our blocks, it makes their jobs a lot easier. We know how to deal with the boys.

But anyway, that day was intense. The kids filed in, one by one, hands behind their backs, heads down, as always. For a while it was actually a pretty uneventful lunch period. No fights, no food thrown, no kids trying to skip the line. I'm guessing because we had pizza.

See, if a student gets in trouble during lunch, they get booted from the cafeteria without a chance to eat, so on days we served a popular dish, they behaved. Everybody loves pizza, right?

So, they ate in silence as usual, the no-talking rule always in effect, when some boys at one table started laughing. I peeked out from the back. I never miss a chance for some comedy.

A teacher went over and gave a warning to the table and then to the kid cracking the jokes. Trey. They all settled down after that. Trey was never one to be bad for *real*.

But maybe five minutes go by and the kids at the table started laughing again. This time because Trey did something with his food, messing around. Bad timing though. Moore walked in.

The teacher went over again and gave Trey a demerit. When the teacher got back to their post, Moore stomped over.

"You having trouble out of that one?" he asked.

"You know it," the teacher replied.

Moore stuck around for a few more minutes, circling the tables, arms crossed, scowling. All the boys sat up straight. He had a spell on us. Or we never wanted any trouble from him when it could be avoided. He took things to the max.

Eventually though, Moore got up to leave, or at least pretended to. And what d'ya know, right on cue, Trey cracked another joke, a loud one, this time about Moore. "Forehead look like a landing strip, boy."

The other kids erupted with laughter until Moore popped his head right back in the cafeteria. And that's when things got interesting. I saw something I've never seen before, something I didn't know was even possible. Moore completely lost his cool.

He stormed across the room. "What you say?"

Trey sure did stay tight-lipped then.

"No, you want to be a clown, then be a clown. Tell a joke," Moore barked.

But Trey kept his mouth shut.

"Tell a *joke*, Jackson!" Moore yelled again.

Trey ignored him again.

When I thought things couldn't get any worse, Moore stooped down in that boy's face and literally yelled, "I said tell a damn joke!"

Some kids snickered, that little laugh to keep from crying type of thing. Others stuffed their mouths full of pizza, terrified.

Trey looked humiliated. Eyes darting all around. He snapped back. "Get the fuck outta my face!"

"Or what?" Moore roared.

"Before I kill you!"

The whole room fell silent. Not even the lunch ladies dared moved. A jolt zipped up my back.

At the time, I didn't think he meant it. Felt more like a defense mechanism. But knowing what I know now . . . I guess that boy was dead-ass serious.

After the shock wore off, Moore grabbed Trey by the collar and pretty much dragged him out the cafeteria.

You know the rest.

Mrs. Hall

Urban Promise Prep Teacher

My poor students. My poor baby boys. I started teaching at Urban Promise the very first year it opened. Been here ever since.

This place used to be magic when those doors first opened. Boys from all across the city who were forgotten about finally had a place to call home. A place where the administration cared about giving them a fair shot. Moore really did. Sure, he'd always been a little strict, but you have to be with these kids, you do. But not out of fear, or hate or misunderstanding—out of love.

Those first couple of years, Urban Promise didn't perform the way we hoped it would, at least not in Moore's eyes. I thought we'd made progress. Sure, we could always be better, but Moore wanted to be the *best*.

So, we went to school visits, conferences, workshops, all sorts of things to learn best practices. A tweak here, a tweak there, and before you know it, I realized we were herding boys like cattle. They weren't kids anymore, they were prisoners.

Recently, I approached Moore about my disapproval with the school culture and do you know he told me to pack up and leave if I didn't like it? He'd changed, a different human entirely from the one

I agreed to work for. Angry. Cold. All the time, all the energy, effort, blood, sweat, and tears I put into that place, and he had the nerve to just . . . toss me aside?!

I'm getting worked up just thinking about it.

Oh, and Trey, a suspect? That boy wouldn't hurt a fly. Talk tough, but I see through that. All these boys talk tough. Give them a little love and watch them melt. They're children. Everyone seems to always forget that. No matter their size. No matter their skin color. No matter their attitude.

Trey never had a fair shake, not even at Promise. It was determined, legally, that he needed an aide in order to do his best learning. But Moore just flat out didn't do it. Said it'd be too costly to hire such a person. Said the school had enough financial troubles as is without taking on more debt. I couldn't believe it.

I don't know exactly what changed Moore. Rumors constantly circulate: infidelity and a disgruntled wife, a messy divorce, talk of a failed investment, some financial trouble he faced.

In any case, the turmoil in his personal life started to bleed into work recently. He'd showed up at school unkempt, late, or even called out sick. He took it out on the kids, even the staff. But I, for one, was tired of being yelled at.

I was there at Promise on the day of the shooting. I'd marched into his office to give him my letter of resignation. I couldn't take it anymore. And when I heard Moore was dead, my first thought was: *Oh God, he did it. He took his own life.*

Trey's Interrogation

(Transcript from Trey's Official Questioning)

DETECTIVE BO: State your name for the record, please.

TREY: Trey.

DETECTIVE ASH: Whole name.

TREY: That is my WHOLE name.

DETECTIVE ASH: You think this shit is funny? Want us to just put you away now?

TREY: Jackson. Trey Jackson.

DETECTIVE BO: Where do you live?

TREY: Southeast, near the Navy Yard.

DETECTIVE BO: Oh, that's right. Your uncle is the former marine.

TREY: You talked to my uncle?

DETECTIVE ASH: We're asking the questions. Where were you on the tenth of October at approximately six thirty P.M.?

TREY: You know where I was.

DETECTIVE BO: Oh, so you were in Moore's office? Gun to his head?

TREY: No, I was in detention. Like I told you a million times.

DETECTIVE BO: Why were you in detention? You a troublemaker?

TREY: C'mon, bruh, do I look like a troublemaker?

DETECTIVE BO: As a matter of fact, you look like the kind of kid who likes to stir shit up.

DETECTIVE ASH: According to teachers at your school, you are.

TREY: That's 'cause teachers don't like me.

DETECTIVE BO: They got to have a reason, right?

TREY: Whatever, man.

DETECTIVE ASH: You hear anything in detention?

TREY: I heard I have rights to a lawyer.

DETECTIVE BO: What do you need a lawyer for? You didn't do anything wrong, right?

TREY: No.

DETECTIVE ASH: Then talk to us, you can trust us. We can help you.

TREY: I don't need your help. I need my lawyer.

DETECTIVE BO: Doesn't matter. You know the other one already told on you.

TREY: Huh? Told what?!

DETECTIVE BO: Told us what you did.

TREY: But I didn't do anything! What they say?

DETECTIVE BO: Not what we heard. Just tell us the truth, from your perspective. Maybe you know something about one of the other kids?

TREY: . . .

DETECTIVE ASH: If you want to play hardball, we can play harder, and you're not going to like it.

TREY: . . .

DETECTIVE ASH: Okay, have it your way.

ONE DAY BEFORE
THE MURDER

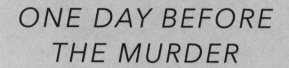

CHAPTER FOUR

Late

TREY

"BOOOOOOY, I'm 'bout to flame you!!" I yell at my boy Brandon, my wingman. He plays the one, I play the two. Plus, he's the only dude on the team that can take my jokes. Probably because Brandon is the coolest kid on the planet, so he never takes anything too personal. "Head look like a PT Cruiser."

The team dies laughing, even Coach. I love getting jokes off in the locker room. Something about the echo makes it sound like the entire school is laughing with me. I wonder what that would sound like, the whole school cracking up at my jokes. That'd be epic. I could be a whole-ass comedian if basketball doesn't work out for me.

"Okay, settle down, y'all, settle down," Coach says. "We got the biggest game of our season tomorrow. This is for all the marbles. We not even thinking about the championship yet, you hear me? This *is* our championship. We leave it all on the floor 'cause if we don't win, we go home. You hear me?"

"Yes, sir!" we shout in unison.

"Great practice today. Y'all get home safely, rest up, and be ready to play tomorrow. All in."

We huddle up and put our hands in the middle. Brandon's the captain so he leads the war cry as usual.

"We got it!"

"WE GOT IT!"

"We ballin'!"

"WE BALLIN'!"

"We got it!"

"WE GOT IT!"

"We Promise!"

"WE PROMISE!!!"

Our hands fly in the air as we break off to the showers.

"Yo, Trey, let me holla' at you," Coach calls out.

I jog over to him. We step behind the last row of lockers, just out of earshot of my teammates.

"Trey, we going to need you tomorrow so get focused, you hear me?"

"Yeah, Coach, I got you."

"My man, that's what I love to hear. Now, go ahead, get cleaned up."

Hearing Coach say the team needs me is the best feeling in the world, especially because basketball's the only thing I'm good at. I don't think I've ever had anybody tell me they need me for anything.

I walk through the blue and gold locker room to the showers where some of the guys are.

"Yo, B," I say to Brandon.

"What did Coach want?" he replies.

"Just told me to be ready for tomorrow."

"You better, we've got a game to win."

"Facts. Let me head out to catch this bus. Tomorrow, Goon."

"Tomorrow, Slime."

Brandon and I do our handshake, and I leave, skipping the shower because I can't miss the very small window to make my bus home.

My Uncle T has a strict rule about the time I get in, and if I'm late by even a couple minutes, that would likely set him off. I don't want any problems with him tonight.

I stop at the first water fountain I see and go to town, mouth dry as hell from practice. We're supposed to only stay at the fountain for three seconds, but since school's out, there isn't anyone around to rush me.

My last school up in the Bronx barely had running water. Drinking fountains never worked, toilets never flushed, sometimes the heat wouldn't even work in the winter, dead-ass. Had me tight. The trade-off, though, was the teachers couldn't care less about what the students did, and I could get away with pretty much whatever I wanted.

Urban Promise is the exact opposite.

Everything is clean, shiny, top of the line. But the amount of BS you have to put up with in this place almost makes it stink.

In class, we can't even lean back in our seat. On top of that, they got the nerve to have us in school from like 7:00 A.M. to 5:00 P.M. Who can sit still like that for ten hours?! I can't. But of course, when I don't sit exactly the way they want me to, I get a warning. Three warnings, then I get a demerit and my count goes down. Once that happened often enough, I became the problem kid that nobody wanted in their class.

That's the one thing that's the same between Promise and my old school. The way the teachers feel about me. The way they look at me. The way they talk to me. The way they talk about me. For some reason, Trey Jackson and schoolteachers just don't get along and I'm always the one to blame.

They'd say things like:

"Trey's one of our *special* students."

"Good luck with that *one*."

Or their personal favorite . . . "He needs a little *extra* love."

All sorts of slick comments.

But I'm not stupid. I know they're speaking in a teacher code, and what they mean to say is:

"We wish Trey wasn't here."

"We wish Trey didn't exist."

I wipe the water from my chin and head to my locker to get my things. Promise is much less stressful after school. No other kids, no nagging teachers. It seems almost normal. I grab the lock on my locker when I hear my name.

I turn around and see Mr. Finley peeking out of his classroom. Pale-ass neck all out, looking like a doggone ostrich.

"Yes?" I try to say politely.

"Why aren't you walking the line?" Mr. Finley asks.

When people ask me stupid questions it always takes me extra-long to answer, so I take a second.

"School's out. There's not even anybody else in the hall."

"So just because nobody's looking you decide to do the wrong thing? What's value four?" He crosses his arms over his chest.

I sigh. "Integrity."

"Where are you coming from?"

"Practice."

"So go back to the gym and try again."

I gasp. "Mr. Finley, you can't be serious. I'mma miss my bus."

"You have to learn to make better choices."

I let out a loud groan he doesn't like and stomp away to bug him even more.

I plant my feet on the line and walk as fast as I can down the hall. I would run but Mr. Finley would just have me do it again and again.

Mr. Finley is famous for making students do stuff over and over.

Torture. I swear, sometimes it just seems like he doesn't like me. Teachers shouldn't be allowed to not like kids.

I look back and of course Mr. Finley is still watching, as if he doesn't have anything else to do, any papers to grade, any parents to call, an apple to eat or whatever it is that teachers pretend to do.

I walk far enough to see the gym and then turn around. I get a glimpse of the hallway clock and see I'm already two minutes later than I need to be, and now I'm stressing. I haven't missed curfew in two weeks, and I don't want to piss Uncle T off the day before a big game. No telling what he might do. I can't have that kind of stress right now. I need to have a perfect game tomorrow, so my head's got to be right.

I don't know what the courts told my uncle about me, but he seems to think I was some big-time troublemaker in New York. I got suspended from school a couple times but I'm not in a gang. I'm not selling drugs like some of my boys back home. I'm just a normal kid.

I rush to my locker, passing Mr. Finley's class on the way. Looks like he left for the day the moment I was out of sight.

I grab my things as fast as possible and dip out the building, heart beating.

Outside, the fresh air feels good hitting my lungs.

But when I turn the corner, my nightmare comes true, and I see the bus pulling away from the stop ahead.

"NO! Wait, wait!" I break out into a full sprint toward the 90. But does the driver hear me?

Of course not. They keep moving.

My stomach drops as I think about what Uncle T will say . . . or do.

CHAPTER FIVE

Stuck

TREY

I get home after the sun goes down, which Uncle T won't like.

Uncle T lives in Southeast right near the Navy Yard. It's a pretty nice area with a stadium nearby and everything. He has a house, so he must be rich, although he doesn't act like it. He's always talking about how much money I cost him. *Turn the lights off when I leave a room, stay away from the thermostat, no seconds at dinner.*

I hold my breath and step inside. I spot him on the living room couch with a beer in his hand, a 211 as always. I try to squeeze to the wall, hoping he somehow won't notice me. I think about that part in *Peter Pan* where Peter fights his shadow. I concentrate on becoming that shadow.

I inch toward the steps when I hear his voice. "Where you been, Trey?" He sounds like a demon.

"Nowhere, I'm just coming from practice."

"Practice ends at six thirty. It only takes an hour to get home. Why is it almost nine o'clock?"

"I missed my bus."

"Why?"

I drop my head.

"It was running ahead of schedule."

"Come here!" he shouts, knowing I'm lying—he always knows.

My feet are like cinder blocks as I make my way toward him. I hate when he tells me to come to him. He gets mad when I move slow, but why would I come to him quickly? I never understand adults.

"Yes?"

"Yes, what?" he snaps.

"Yes, sir?"

"You lying to me, boy?"

"No, si—" Before I can even finish, I feel the breath leave my body. My chest seems to touch my spine and my feet involuntarily take three steps back.

I hate being punched in the chest.

But even more, I hate that no matter what I say, Uncle T already has his mind made up about me. Just like those teachers down at Promise.

Moving to DC from New York and going to Promise changed my life in a bunch of ways. Mostly good. Back home in the Bronx, I didn't see my mom much. The freedom was cool for a while, but then she started bringing strange dudes home all the time. It got really weird for me a few times and I wanted out.

When the city said I couldn't live with her anymore, I was relieved. When I found out Uncle T was taking me in, I felt happy. I thought Uncle T was pretty cool from the few times I'd met him. He had a Cadillac and that was dope to me, but when he became my guardian, I saw a different side.

Uncle T has a serious drinking problem. I know he was a marine, and I think sometimes he still thinks he is. He does the same thing every day. Goes to work, exercises, drinks beer, watches TV, and cleans his gun. And when he isn't doing those things, he's bossing me around. It's almost like he's training me for the military too. He calls it discipline, that he's shaping me into a man.

Sometimes I think about hitting him back, but always chicken out when I see his muscles.

"You better not be lying, Trey," he says.

"I'm not, sir. I missed my bus."

"Why?"

I search for an answer other than the truth. I can't say I got in trouble for not walking in the hall correctly, because that'll only prove it was my fault.

"Practice ran a little over. We got a big game tomorrow."

When I remind him of my basketball game, I see his face relax. He likes that I'm good at basketball.

"That is tomorrow, isn't it?"

I nod. He sighs. Closest thing to an apology he ever gives.

"Why didn't you say that at first, Trey?"

"I don't know, I just remembered."

He shakes his head at me.

"Sit down for a second."

I plop down on the opposite end of the couch. As far away as I can.

"You know, I'm tough on you for a reason. I don't want to see you go down the path your mother did."

He gets on these drunk rants where he says mean things so easily, like they won't hurt my feelings.

"In fact, I even invited an old friend from the navy," he continues, "to come check you out. See about getting you a scholarship to go there."

I hate the navy. Their colors suck.

"Thanks, Uncle T," I say.

"You thank me by showing up tomorrow, you hear me?"

"Yes, sir."

"Good, now there's some TV dinners in the kitchen. Eat up."

I sulk out the living room and head to my room. Skip dinner.

The faster I go to sleep, the faster tomorrow will come. And all I can think about is playing in that basketball game.

Yeah. Things will be better tomorrow.

THE DAY OF THE MURDER

Trey

CHAPTER SIX

Trouble!

TREY

I almost jump out of my skin when my phone alarm goes off.

I hop out of bed and throw on the same uniform from yesterday, for the sake of time. If I'm late to school, that's an automatic detention. That's a no go, I'm not missing this basketball game for nothing.

I look around for my book bag but don't see it. At Promise, if you come to school without a book bag, they won't even let you in. That happens enough times, they expel you.

I run to the living room and see my bag by the couch. I scoop it up on the way out the door. Luckily, Uncle T's already out on his morning run.

I jog down the street praying I didn't miss the bus again, but after the day I had yesterday, it's no telling what might happen. When I turn the corner, people are loading onto the bus about two blocks away. I start to freak out until I notice an old lady in a wheelchair at the back of the line. That's going to buy me some time.

I quicken my pace, jaywalk a couple of intersections and sure enough, I run up just as the bus finishes loading.

Some good luck on the day of one of the biggest basketball games of my career. I start running plays in my head, mentally rehearsing all that me and Brandon worked on. I imagine the last play of the game, an assist from Brandon and a game-winning shot by me. Or maybe it's the other way around, maybe I toss him the rock and he gets that final bucket. Either way, we got each other's backs, and that feels good.

When we pull up across the street from Promise I press the button on the back door of the bus and wait for the thing to slow to a stop. Once it does, the doors open, and I'm off.

As I walk toward Promise, I look for my school ID while thinking back to Coach saying he needed me. If I do well today, I'll make him proud. I think about my uncle's friend from the navy, and how I have a chance to make Uncle T proud of me too. I think about how Brandon is going to make his mom and dad proud.

I can't find my ID in my pockets, so I search my book bag. When I look inside my jaw drops.

Holy. Shit.

Instead of my ID, or my gym clothes, or my textbooks . . . I'm staring at Uncle T's pistol. I remember I left my book bag by the couch, right by Uncle T's. They look the same and I must've taken his by accident.

My stomach twists and my heart feels like it's going to burst.

I'm buggin'! I can't go to school with this, I'll be arrested at the metal detectors!

I can't go back home, I'll miss half of school, no way I'll be able to play in the game if that happens. I wish I could just call Uncle T, tell him I made a mistake and ask him to help me. But that ain't my life. He's going to think I took it. He doesn't give me the benefit of the doubt. He doesn't do mistakes or excuses.

What the hell am I going to do?

PART THREE

Ramón

Present Day

Rachel Barnes

Older Sister to Anthony Barnes, Urban Promise Prep Student

I do think one of those kids is guilty. And it ain't the Black ones.

You know I live in the same neighborhood as Ramón, in Columbia Heights? I see him from time to time with some of the local guys, *real* gang types. The scary ones. Dioses del Humo.

Dioses del Humo is big in my neighborhood, and they don't play, let me tell you. Murder is not an issue. Every other day I flip on the news, there's some gang violence at their hands. I knew street guys growing up, but they're different. It's like they *like* murdering.

Recently I started seeing Ramón kicking it with them more and more, and at first I didn't think much of it. Then a few weeks ago, I saw Ramón's cousin pick him up from school when I went to get my brother.

Ramón's older cousin is a leader in the gang.

I'm no snitch or nothing, but being a concerned community member and all, I thought it'd be good to tell Moore, just as a precaution. They certainly don't need none of that mess up in Urban Promise Prep. I mean, my brother goes there. I need him safe.

Moore said he would look into it. I didn't think much of it after that, but then, the day before Moore was killed, I saw Ramón's older cousin getting arrested in front of the school.

Moore was the type to go to any lengths to protect these boys, and I do mean *any*.

And the next day, Moore was killed.

So I think Ramón did this in retaliation. To a man that was trying to save him from himself.

Like I said, with them, murder ain't an issue.

Anthony "Tony" Barnes

Urban Promise Prep Student

H ere's the thing about Promise—you either love it or you hate it. If you love it, you play by the rules and everything is fine. If you hate it—well, I don't know. I'm the kind of person who tries to use what I have to get what I want. And even if I don't go to college, graduating from Promise looks good in this city. I really want to do something with my hands—welding like my dad. Don't tell my sister Rachel I said that. She's all about college, and so is Promise.

"It's the only way to get what you want, Tony! You take care of Promise, it will take care of you." And I guess she's right . . . Principal Moore does take care of us, in his way. But there's more than one way to get what you want.

Ramón is the perfect example, even if Rachel thinks he's bad news. It's one thing to see him around the neighborhood. It's rough sometimes. But if she was actually at Promise she would be able to see what she can't see back home.

We call him Chef Ramón. I mean, the guy can cook! If it wasn't for Ramón, you'd have to be uptown to taste his abuelita's pupusas, but Ramón got smart and hustles them at school. On the low, obviously, because Moore doesn't tolerate any of that.

But man, we want to eat right, and the cafeteria staff is stretched thin. All this donation money from rich people and politicians, but still the only thing Moore hasn't shut down yet is the cooking initiative where seniors help out in the kitchen. Even Rachel admits that's because Moore doesn't want to spend the money to hire more lunch staff.

The other teachers are always complaining about it. I overheard them gossiping about how there's other things the school is supposed to be spending money on too, but Moore thinks that cash should go somewhere else. And that man holds the key to the castle, no one else. I sure as hell don't know where that money is going, though.

Chef Ramón didn't only make fire pupusas, he makes other things too. Always experimenting. Sometimes he'll slide you a sample on the blue line. It seems like good business. He has his friend Luis to help him too. If I was making all the money that Ramón was making, I'd be wearing new kicks all the time. But Ramón said the money was for his abuelita and her store, plus his *stash*. Whatever that means.

Either way, I never thought he was as bad as Rachel thinks.

Me and Ramón happened to be walking out of school at the same time one day and she basically grabbed me by the ear thinking I was joining Dioses del Humo right there on the steps of Promise. That's not even how it works.

Rachel has a lot on her plate. Our parents work two and three jobs so she ends up doing a lot of parent-type stuff—calling about conferences and things like that. Sometimes I think she's a little too serious.

But maybe she had the right idea. Now with Principal Moore dead, I feel weird about being back at Promise. Everything that happened before feels significant: like Moore shutting down all Ramón's food sales. *We're building men, making kings, not punks!* I don't know why Moore did that.

I've spent a lot of time since Moore was murdered connecting dots. When I think about what Ramón said that day—that he was saving money for his stash—I wonder what he meant. Was he selling drugs? Somebody said the shooter hid the gun at Promise.

Who knows what Ramón had stashed? What if I helped him pay for a gun by buying pupusas? Does that make me an accessory to murder?

Please don't tell Rachel.

César

Ramón's Cousin

I don't have anything to say.

Because I know how people twist my words. If I say I loved my primo, it will get turned into *I used his love to make him do . . .* If I say we weren't close, it'll get turned into *He's lying for Ramón because they're in a gang together. Bangers always cover for each other.*

It's no secret who I am. You want me to say it? I don't need to. My tattoos speak for themselves. That's why I got them—so I am known. Only takes a day in this world to learn that people will see you the way they want to see you, then do what they want to do. At least with these tattoos, some things are crystal clear. I know who is with me, and who is against me.

That's more than my primo can say, isn't it? His abuela put him in that school to keep him safe, right? How safe is he now? He ended up in trouble just like he might've if he was in the streets. The only difference is everyone is so much more shocked because it happened *somewhere like Promise.*

I've seen news cameras in my neighborhood, sweeping down the street to show broken windows and dudes on corners. I've seen the same kind of footage on TV of the halls of Promise—both look at us like animals; they just see one set as tame.

But as rich as those halls look, those people don't understand that when you put poor boys in a school, you can't expect them to become something they're not. I'm no fancy principal, but even I know that don't make sense. When you need money, when you need to survive, violence follows. The only difference between me and them boys at Promise is the uniform we wear. They have theirs and I have mine, but we all the same. Lions in a jungle, fighting to be king.

Doña Gloria

Ramón's Abuela

My Ramón did not do this.

When these things happen to brown boys, they always put their faces on the television and find the one photo in a thousand that makes them look like criminals. But if that was true of Ramón, it would mean I didn't know my grandson at all.

But I did. I do. Deep in my heart.

My grandson is soft like dough. My grandson is sweet like honey. He did not do this. He rises without being asked to help me make pupusas. He asks me how to make all the meals I remember from my girlhood without me prompting. Every child has dreams until the world crushes them out of him. But the world had not crushed the dreams out of my Ramón yet. No, no yet, despite its best efforts.

People have their beliefs about what emigrating is like. There's this idea that it's easy, that picking up and leaving your home and starting over somewhere new is easy; that learning English is easy. It's not. Leaving El Salvador and coming here was hard work. And it's even harder with an older child, like Ramón was when he arrived. We struggled to learn this language, especially him. I could see the strain it put on him, even as a little boy. The shame. Shame can grow into anger.

Yes, he got detention. But that's always the word that travels fast: *detention. Trouble. Suspension. Expulsion.* What travels slower is the truth: detention for selling pupusas at school. In trouble for *laughing*. Suspension for selling food without permission. Yes, he had been told not to. So, he set up a sale in the cafeteria. He found a way to do what he loved by staying within the rules. Promise always said they rewarded innovation.

Where I come from, men laugh and dance and hug each other. It's our culture. Why does Principal Moore want to strip it away?

I will tell you the truth: I thought long and hard about taking Ramón out of that place. Ramón had become so tense lately. My sweet boy, angry like his tío could be. We didn't see his uncle often. But he saw enough of César, and I think Ramón knew that was a path he should stay away from.

I never had to tell him that. He just knew.

But that didn't stop César from staying after Ramón about joining the Dioses del Humo. César must've realized the Dioses were not going to leave Ramón alone. Sometimes a wolf can only protect another wolf if they're in a pack together. Otherwise, the pack turns on you. But that's the thing—my Ramón is not a wolf. He's a gentle boy! I even had to be the one to tell him to be ready to defend himself against whoever hurt him.

There were days he would be fuming and upset about that school. He was saving money for a storefront. His dreams don't even fit in this house, not even in this whole city. He was doing what he had to do to reach them. One day he came home red-faced, and tears were in his eyes. I asked him what happened and all he said was

"Moore . . ." but then he stopped. He told me I had enough to worry about.

Why don't children know that the only thing that matters to us is them? That all the other worries are small, easily put away? I couldn't get it out of him, and now here we are.

I told him to defend himself, no matter who hurt him.

Magdalena Peña

Ramón's Cousin

The thing about being the sister of a boy like César is that everyone also treats you as his mother. *Why can't you make him stop? Why don't you talk to him?* If people knew César like I know César, they would know that he has built this fortress around himself with all the things that have hurt him, and nothing in the world will ever make him come out of it until he's ready. Not his mother, not his father, and not me. So, I stay away from him, which makes me sad. But I always text him and let him know that I'm here for him, whenever he's ready to talk.

I think Ramón knows exactly what that's like. Besides my parents, Ramón is the only one who loves César as much as I do. He knows how it is to have someone you love hurt you inside. People see César and they see Dioses del Humo. When they see the Dioses, they think guns, razor blades. But guns and razor blades are fast and brutal. There are other, slower, and more agonizing ways you can hurt people.

Sometimes Ramón would come home late from helping Abuelita at the shop. He always wore a black T-shirt when he wasn't at Promise, and it would be dirtied, covered in small, dried-up chunks of dough. He had to pass our house to get to his house, and this is usually when he and César would stop and talk for a while. This was one of the only times they were ever really one-on-one—usually when César talked to anybody, the other Dioses were with him, and that made the conversation very different.

Those nights are some of the only times I saw César relax and laugh. Ramón could always make him laugh. Sometimes our neighbor, Don José, would poke his head out and call to them, and they'd all laugh. Don José has known us all for years. He's one of the few people outside our family who doesn't act scared of César.

As much as Ramón looked up to César, though, they did argue sometimes. One night when I went out there to listen, César kept saying, "Why do you think I would do something to steer you wrong? I know you're struggling! Let me help you!"

And Ramón would just shake his head over and over until César got a little loud and said, "Do you think I'm a bad guy, huh? Do you think my brothers are bad guys?" and eventually Ramón yelled, "Yes! I do!"

They argued that night. But that was before Moore got César arrested. Word spread down the block and suddenly everything felt different when I saw Ramón. The pressure was already too much, but now it felt like he was at a breaking point. Don José told my mother that he saw Ramón on the corner with some Dioses the day César was arrested. Said they looked to be pumping Ramón up, and that for the first time, it looked like Ramón was comfortable.

The last text I got from Ramón the day before Moore was killed was this:

> What do you do when you run out of options? When it feels like all the people you're supposed to trust have shown you they can't be trusted?

Even now, I don't know if he was talking about Moore or César.

Nobody

Urban Promise Prep Student

Rumor has it that the killer had been showing signs of being ready to snap.

But no one is ever looking at the right person.

They're distracted by all the other noise.

Ramón's Interrogation

(Transcript from Ramón's Official
Questioning)

DETECTIVE BO: State your name for the record.

RAMÓN: Ramón. Ramón Antonio Torres Zambrano.

DETECTIVE BO: That's a lot of names.

RAMÓN: Yeah. I guess, if you're not Latino.

DETECTIVE ASH: You've been really cooperative so
    far. We appreciate that. We want you to know
    it's safe to tell us the truth.

DETECTIVE BO: No matter what you did, we can make
    sure you're taken care of.

RAMÓN: I told you, I didn't do anything.

DETECTIVE BO: Ramón. Ramón. It's okay. We're on
    your side here. Principal Moore was on your
    back a lot.

DETECTIVE ASH: I couldn't handle it if somebody was
    on my back like that all the time. I'd probably
    snap.

RAMÓN: I didn't kill Principal Moore. I was in
    detention. I wouldn't kill nobody.

DETECTIVE BO: Let's cut the shit, kid. You wouldn't kill anybody? I don't think you end up running with the Dioses del Humo unless the opposite is true.

RAMÓN: I'm not a Dios! Don't talk about things you don't know about.

DETECTIVE BO: Temper, temper. Sounding a little like your cousin there.

RAMÓN: You don't know shit about my primo.

DETECTIVE ASH: I knew he had a little hot streak, Bo, didn't I?

DETECTIVE BO: You sure called it. Watch your mouth, kid. Right now we're both being nice, but that can stop at any time. And believe me, kid, you do *not* want that to happen.

RAMÓN: I'm not saying nothing else.

DETECTIVE ASH: Look, let's all relax, how's that? We'll make sure you're taken care of. You want to make sure your grandma is safe, right?

RAMÓN: What's wrong with my abuela?

DETECTIVE BO: Nothing . . . yet. But you know how it is with the Dioses. Nobody is safe. They hear you're here, talking with us, they might get the wrong idea.

RAMÓN: But I'm not talking. I'm not saying nothing.

DETECTIVE BO: So you do know something.

RAMÓN: Huh? You're confusing me! Stop talking to me!

DETECTIVE ASH: Look, if you can give us what we need, we can maybe cut a deal with you for

Moore. Make sure you're out sooner so you can make sure Abuela is safe too.

RAMÓN: I didn't do anything! Why does everybody think I'm a Dios? I didn't do nothing with them and I didn't do nothing to Moore! Get out of my face!

DETECTIVE ASH: So, you didn't care that Moore had your cousin arrested?

RAMÓN: I didn't say I didn't care. And I told you don't talk about my primo!

DETECTIVE BO: There's that temper again! You're pretty mad—you must have been pretty mad then too.

RAMÓN: I was mad, but—

DETECTIVE ASH: I don't know about you, Bo, but when I get mad, I sometimes do things I'm not so proud of later.

DETECTIVE BO: Oh, me too. You were mad, Ramón. It's human. So, what did the Dioses del Humo say? Are they the ones that helped you get the gun or did you manage that on your own?

RAMÓN: I've never fired a gun. I've never even *held* a gun!

DETECTIVE ASH: Ramón, come on. I find that very hard to believe. In your neighborhood?

RAMÓN: Why won't you believe me?!

DETECTIVE ASH: Kid, your property was found at the scene of the crime. It's time to come clean.

RAMÓN: I was in detention!

DETECTIVE BO: We can do this all day, Ramón. And believe me, we'll find out the truth, whatever it takes.

ONE DAY BEFORE
THE MURDER

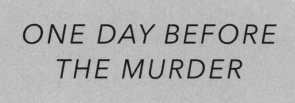

CHAPTER SEVEN

Guilty

RAMÓN

eep beep.

B My dreams are always cut short. It's because I don't get good sleep. Every night is loud in my neighborhood. Police cars, ambulances, fire trucks, honking cars, helicopters, you name it. There's never any quiet, and there certainly isn't any peace. In fact, where I find peace most is at school. At Promise.

My abuela was so happy to get me into that school. The farther away from my primo César, the better. She loves him as much as she loves me, but it's a disappointed kind of love. Maybe if he was as close with her as I am, that disappointment could sway his decisions. I know I could never do anything that would make her look at me the way she looks at César. Either way, we're family. She loves us all.

But me and Abuela have always been the closest. We had to be, I guess. It's not just that we live together. We have so much in common.

Where would I be if I wasn't cooking with my abuela? All my future dreams are made of masa.

But the beeping of my alarm wakes me up just as I was starting to fall into a deep slumber, killing any chance for dreaming today. As I slowly get up I have to shake the frustration that creeps its way into my bones. Instead, I remember why I'm waking up so early, to spend extra time with Abuela and help her prep stuff for the shop. Every morning I find her waiting in the kitchen, already started.

But today she doesn't want me to help. She shoos me out of the kitchen.

"No, no, not today," she says. "It's going to rain. Your bus is always late when it's raining so you need to get on an earlier one."

"Abuela—"

"Go, go! You can't be late for school—you may miss something!"

Abuela takes school extremely seriously. She didn't have a chance to attend college in El Salvador. She sees Promise as an opportunity for me, one that I should take advantage of. I see it that way too I guess, as long as I graduate.

I mean, don't get me wrong, I do okay at Promise. But I've heard of people in their senior year getting put out because they couldn't cut it. Sometimes I feel guilty about the things I keep from her. Like if I get a bad score on an exam or if I get detention. Sometimes I even avoid telling her about parent-teacher conferences so she can't get my report from school. Lying to her hurts me, but I do it anyway.

For example, I told her my bus is what has made me late to school, but that isn't true at all. It's that sometimes I get off at another stop and walk around Adams Morgan to look at my future restaurant. I mean, it's just a dream right now. But as long as the storefront stays empty, it almost feels like it's just waiting for me. Waiting for me to graduate. Waiting for me to go to a top culinary school. Waiting for me to bring all my dreams to life.

I kiss Abuela on the cheek, even as I feel the guilt sink in my stomach. Because she's right—I should go straight to school. But the storefront calls me. I walk toward the bus stop, and the guilt starts to melt away as it gets replaced with excitement.

Beep beep.

A nearby bus, not mine, is lowering its ramp so an old man can get on without too much hassle. He's probably somebody's abuelo and needs help, and I wish I had the time. I shake my head to get the beeps out. That's when I hear someone call my name.

"Primo, don't you hear me?"

My heart sinks. I know that voice. But out here on the block, it sounds a lot different from when we talk one-on-one in the privacy of our home.

"Hey, César," I say, turning toward him. He lopes up the block toward me, his hands in his pockets. He doesn't smile much these days. I remember him being so happy when we were little kids.

"You should know better than to ignore me," he says. His mouth smirks, but his eyes don't smile. I can tell he's demanding the truth— was I ignoring him? This is who my cousin becomes during the day— the leader of the Dioses first, my cousin second.

"I didn't hear you," I say. "Just focused on getting to school."

"Then where you walking to? Ain't your bus stop that way?" He nods down the street.

"Uh, just taking a little detour. Got something I want to see."

"A girl?"

"No, not a girl."

My cousin looks around. "Well, be careful, some shit went down the other day and there could be retaliation."

I just nod. I hate that César's choices affect the whole family, but I know he'd do anything to protect all of us. And I mean anything.

He studies me, and I feel all my muscles tightening up. He's going to ask. He always asks.

"You're out here by yourself," he says, scowling. "You'd be safer with us. You need to be smart and get with me and the Dioses."

"Don't worry about me, primo. I'm just going to school."

"You just said you *weren't* going to school," he says, and his eyes glint.

"I *am* going to school. I'm just going somewhere else first."

César looks at me, squinting the way he does when he's looking at somebody he doesn't trust.

"Okay, I'm just making sure you straight. We family."

We are family. In a lot of ways, César has been more like my big brother than my cousin. And in that way, Magda, César's younger sister, is like my sister too. That's one thing me and César definitely have in common, we're both very protective of Magdalena. I told her once that I think that's part of the reason César is so down with the Dioses—because he knows that every guy in the crew is down to ride for Magda. I would too.

"What's in the bag?" he demands.

"School stuff."

"I smell pupusas. You still pushing those?"

I feel my face heat up. It's not that I'm embarrassed of cooking—especially not with César. He actually used to cook with me when we were little kids. He liked making sweet stuff, though. And was good at it too. I just think he'll see cooking as one more thing I spend time doing instead of joining him and the Dioses.

"Yeah," I admit.

César smirks. "You got some horchata in there too?" he says, grabbing at my bag.

"No jodás," I say, pulling away.

When he sees I'm not kidding around, he straightens up. Guys like César respect when you stand up for yourself. It shows you have heart.

"Okay, okay, you have your own little hustle, then, I see," he says, and for a brief second I can tell César is proud of me. The way he looks at me makes me feel like it's just us out on the street. But the moment only lasts for that brief second, because out here, eyes are always watching.

"Yeah I do. In fact, I'm going to open my own storefront . . ."

I didn't mean to say it out loud. I got caught up in the moment, too comfortable. As soon as the words leave my mouth, César bursts out laughing.

"A storefront? Like a restaurant?"

"Yeah," I say, now embarrassed. "Eventually."

He laughs even harder. It used to bother me before, but now I'm used to people laughing at my dreams. Sharing your dreams with folks from the hood was always risky because most people don't believe in the same possibilities I do. Still, coming from César it feels more painful. A scowl takes over my own mouth.

"Whatever," I say. "I'm out." I start to walk away, but I realize I have more to say, so I turn back around.

"You know, you could be helping me and Abuela. She *always* needs help with selling the food. I'm going to go to school and learn the right way to do business—"

César cuts me off. "You think going to school makes you better than me? What's the right way to do business? 'Cause I got some info the school won't teach you, but the streets will, and that ain't no 'right way' in this world. Everybody just out for self. Soft-ass school made you think that the world is good and that if you work hard enough, your dreams will come true." He shakes his head. "People where we from don't own restaurants, primo. You know anybody in the hood with the cash to buy a building? Legal cash? Yeah, we're gonna help Doña Elena and Don Marco since they had that fire, and whoever else in the neighborhood that needs it. But we're not out here trying to be angels. We just tryna' make it."

My chest feels tight. I make sure I keep my voice from trembling.

"And who says we can't own things, huh? Why don't you think I can have my own restaurant?"

My face feels hotter than ever. He's like a big brother and I've always felt like a little boy when I talk to César. But today, I feel like an old man, trying to reason with another old man—like we're both just stuck in our ways.

"We can," he answers. "But it doesn't look like going to school and trying to fit into some shit that hates us in the first place. We have to work together to build our own. This is the only choice *they* leave us with."

I understand the words he's saying, I just don't agree. I don't see life as only one choice. But then again, I'm not in his shoes. Maybe for him, there really is just one option.

"If you tell yourself there's only one choice, that's all you'll see, primo. And that's something I learned at school."

A red Dodge Hellcat rolls up beside us, brakes squeaking. For a second my heart jumps but César seems calm, so I settle down. The window rolls down and it's Ever, César's second-in-command.

"Yo, fool, shit already jumping."

I look at Ever, but I can feel César's eyes burning into me. Ever nods to me and I nod back.

"We can finish this conversation later," César says.

I hold my breath, truly hoping there is a later.

I've always looked the other way when César and the Dioses do what they do. I've heard the rumors of what happens when they settle their beef. I know how the other Dioses look at César—and what he had to do to earn that respect.

"Yeah, sure, I'll see you," I say, rushing up the street.

I try to forget what just happened and keep my focus on getting to my future shop.

But when I get to the front of the building, my mouth drops.

There's no longer a FOR SALE sign in the window. In fact, it's a SOLD sign. My heart sinks. I notice a smaller sign on the front door and step up to read it.

COMING SOON: ASIAN-MEXICAN FUSION IS ON ITS WAY! THIS SAN FRAN-CISCO CHEF IS EXCITED ABOUT HIS NEW SPACE.

The preview image shows a white guy in a chef's hat, grinning and holding chopsticks and a crunchy taco shell. That's all it takes for my heart to stop sinking and start flaming. It's not even that I actually thought I would be the one to lease that place and open my restaurant. But . . . I kind of did. Dreams don't have sense. I stare at the guy in the picture. *Asian-Mexican fusion.* If I keep looking, I'm going to smash this fucking window. So, I walk away as fast as possible instead.

My bus pulls up and I dig out my SmarTrip card and climb on, feeling even more tired than before. The bus driver grumbles and I move my way to the back of the bus, my eyes on the seat I'm aiming for. Something catches my eye though as I move back—a familiar face.

Mr. Reggie.

He's a security guard at school, and without meaning to I hear in my head *beep beep beep.* Almost like he can give me a demerit here on the bus. Hell, maybe he can. With this stupid Promise uniform I have on, I know he notices me. How could this day get any worse?!

Mr. Reggie and I had a run-in before. Last week, someone had the nerve to snitch on me to him about selling pupusas. I couldn't believe that.

Anyway, Mr. Reggie then had to search my locker and turn so-called "contraband" over to Principal Moore, even though he didn't seem to want to do it. Somehow Moore had that power over teachers and faculty, where they'd do things they didn't even believe in, just to satisfy Moore. I don't hate Promise like some of the other kids, but it can be too much at times.

I move to the back of the bus where Mr. Reggie can't stare at me the whole ride. I take out my phone and text Magda.

> **Ramón:** I just ran into César at the bus stop.

Magda: Ugh. I'm already on my way to school, otherwise I would have yelled at him to leave you alone. I'm sorry.

> **Ramón:** Did he say anything to you about only having one choice??

Magda: Huh?

> **Ramón:** I don't know, he was acting kind of weird. Like he wanted to talk to me about something, but didn't get a chance. I couldn't tell if it was a bad thing or not.

Magda: Well, you never know with him. Is everything okay with you? I heard you got busted selling pupusas and stuff at school.

> **Ramón:** Damn everything gets out at Promise!! How did you even hear about it?

Magda: Do you really want to know?

Ramón: Of course

Magda: That little rat Becca was talking about it in class yesterday.

Magda goes to Mercy too, that all-girl school not far from Promise. The students there are super smart, smarter than the boys at Promise. But sometimes they act a way, looking down on us. Of course, Magda is so different from the other girls at Mercy.

"Ain't this your stop?" someone calls, and I jerk my head up, realizing they're talking to me. It's Mr. Reggie, the security guard, standing at the back door of the bus, staring at me with an ugly look on his face. "You're not skipping school, are you?"

"N-no," I stutter. The pressure of Mr. Reggie staring at me makes me nervous. If he catches me with these pupusas I'm finished. I'll get detention before I even make it to school.

I hope he doesn't mistake my anxiety for guilt.

"Well, this is the stop if you're *actually* going to school," he says.

"I am," I say. "I was just daydreaming, I guess."

"Uh-huh, that's you kids' problem these days. Always on your phone or got your head in the clouds. Come on," Mr. Reggie mutters, waiting for me to get off before he begins walking. "Always trying to get away with something."

I have no choice but to follow him all the way to school, and my abuela was right—it starts to rain. I don't have an umbrella, but I put my book bag up over my head, trying to stay a little dry. Mr. Reggie glances back at me from under his umbrella. The thought doesn't occur to him to offer me refuge. But why would it?

By the time we climb the stairs of Promise, the rain is pouring down and we duck inside.

"Head straight to study hall," Mr. Reggie grumbles, shaking off his umbrella. "I don't know why you wanted to come to school all early."

There's no point in arguing. I turn toward the study hall room, raindrops dripping off my backpack. I look behind me and see a trail of water. Maybe I'm petty, but I smirk. I look around to make sure I'm all alone before unzipping my book bag. I peek inside and my pupusa supply is okay despite the bad weather.

I'm almost to the room when I hear someone cursing. Not cursing someone out, but the way my abuela does when she can't find her car keys. Except this person is cursing in English, low and growling, but loud enough for me to hear. I walk softer, surprised anybody is here. The office is dark. My heart sinks, thinking it's Moore. I will definitely get a demerit if he sees me dripping all over the hall. I try to walk faster.

But when I pass the office, Dean Hicks steps out and runs right into me.

"Where are you supposed to be?" he shouts. His voice is almost as big as Moore's. I flinch. "Why are you even here at this hour?"

"I'm sorry, sir," I try. "I took the wrong bus. Mr. Reggie told me I could go to . . ."

I hate when this happens. I know what I want to say. But when I'm anxious, it's like all the English words fly out of my head.

"Go where?" he demands.

"Um, go to . . . to . . ."

"YES?"

"Study hall," I say. So simple. How does it disappear?

"Well, what are you doing here, then?" he demands. "Skulking about in the hall? That's a demerit."

Beep beep beep.

I don't know the word *skulk*. But it sounds like one of those words that means what it sounds like. Makes me think of *skunk*. Or *sneak*. I am neither of those things and I feel myself get mad. But there's no room for getting mad here. I just nod and make my way away from the dark office.

Outside the rain is pouring down and it's loud against the roof with the school this quiet. When I sink down into the seat and take off my blazer, all I can hear is rain. With the high ceiling, it sounds far away. Maybe I can dry off before school starts in an hour. Maybe I can get some work done, or at least daydream about my restaurant in peace.

I think maybe this day can turn around.

CHAPTER EIGHT

Police

RAMÓN

After the morning I'd had, I felt a little bit of hope when I sold all the pupusas for the day. My bag was light, and my pockets were full, and aside from feeling slightly damp all day from the rain, things were okay. I head to my locker, put away what I don't need, grab what I do, and walk outside, where the rain has stopped. Everything is fine until I see a car I recognize.

César's car, silver and shiny, with César hanging out the window smiling at me as I come down the steps of Promise. Why is he *here*? A mix of worry and surprise bubble up inside me. I gaze around for Principal Moore. Among his many rules were ones about known gang members being on school grounds. The whole community took it very seriously. I didn't think I'd see him again so soon. César picked me up a few weeks ago, and I saw Moore take note, so I told him not to come here again. I didn't need any extra attention on me.

"Primo," he calls as I walk over to the car slowly. I see guys checking the car out, clocking César and me. I know they know who César is. Some of them just stare, some of them frown, some look afraid. My heart hammers. I hope Moore doesn't see us.

"What are you doing here?"

"I said I'd catch you later. How's business? Did you sell all those pupusas?"

I nod, but I don't move to walk around the other side of the car to get in. He notices my hesitation and his smile fades.

"What's the problem?"

"I just . . . what are you doing here, César?"

César pauses. "I just wanted you to show me the storefront," he says. "Your little restaurant dream spot you were talking about. Figured it would be faster to drive than take the bus."

I drop my head and the disappointment of my shop selling runs through me.

"Maybe you were right. Maybe we can't own things like that. The shop sold. Some white guy from the West Coast."

"Well, that's what I wanted to talk about," he says. He looks at his steering wheel instead of me, almost scowling. "Maybe I was wrong. I thought about what you said. Maybe there's another option here. Another storefront, you know?"

A warm feeling comes over me. César, the big brother I never had. He always knows the right thing to say when I find myself in a shitty situation.

"For sure." I smile, suddenly getting excited. "Let's go to Adams Morgan; we can drive around and see what else is available."

"Sounds good, little cousin, hop in."

Right as I reach for the car door, the air fills with the sound of sirens. Red and blue lights flash from all angles. I see my face reflected in César's: both of us shocked, confused, scared.

Three cop cars roll up on us, one at each end of César's car, and one right in the middle, stopping inches from T-boning his ride.

"Hands where we can see them! Step out of the car!"

Cops jump out of all the cars; some of them even have guns. I don't think people know how terrifying it is to have a gun pointed at you. It's even worse when it's a cop because unlike a robbery or something, you know that the person in the uniform can do whatever they want and nobody will say anything. When *that* gun is pointed at you, it's scarier because *that* gun isn't bound by the same rules.

"Out of the car! Now step away! Hands on your head!"

Everything happens so fast, and also so slow. They throw César on the ground. One jerks me to the side, dragging me up onto the grass of Promise. They swarm his car, searching in all the pockets and seats. César is on the ground with a knee on his back and a hand shoving his face into the concrete.

"César, what's happening?! Let me go! César!" I struggle in the cop's arms.

"Found something!" shouts one of the cops searching César's car. He withdraws his hand from the passenger side, something metal and shiny in his grip.

A gun.

"That ain't mine!" César yells.

"Looks like it to me," says the cop whose knee is in his back. He shoves the back of my cousin's head, knocking his jaw hard into the concrete. César struggles and the cop does it again. I should be shouting, but all my words dry up.

They ask me questions and search me too, but it's obvious that César is who they came for. I'm not sure how they knew he'd be here. Were they following him? Did someone snitch?

I watch them haul César into the back of a cruiser, blood on his chin. I take a shaky step forward but a cop shoves me back with both arms.

"Don't tell Magda!" César shouts at me before they slam the door in his face.

I stand watching as the cops all pile back into their cars. A police tow truck pulls up at some point and yanks César's car up into the air. In a few minutes, it's like we were never there at all.

I don't care who's around to see—my eyes fill with tears. But when I look up at the school, I can see through them very easily. Principal Moore on the steps, arms crossed over his chest, nodding, as if to say, *Perfect*.

THE DAY OF THE MURDER

Ramón

CHAPTER NINE

Some Get Back

RAMÓN

I spent all night planning.

Stayed up late getting it all together, trying to focus the rage that built inside me like a bonfire. Abuela even helped me. Four hands are better than two, she said. And she was right. With her help with proportions, I made quadruple the amount of pupusas I would usually take to school and packed them all into my backpack, plus another extra lunch bag.

Between this and what Abuela can bring home from working at the bakery, we should be able to pool our money with Tío's and bail out César. Abuela doesn't approve of what César does, but I told her everything that happened, how Principal Moore specifically called the cops on César when my primo wasn't doing anything wrong. Rarely does Abuela criticize a teacher or school staff, but even that made her lips narrow. And she definitely isn't going to let her nephew sit in jail.

My bags sag heavy with the food as I make my way to the bus stop. I won't be getting on the other bus today and risk Mr. Reggie seeing me. I find myself eyeing the windows of every passing one. Going to Promise is starting to make me feel paranoid.

I'm still standing there fuming when someone grabs my shoulder, and I'm so fired up that I whirl around, dropping the pupusa bag and raising my fist.

"Easy, kid," the guy who grabbed me says, putting his hands up to show he means no harm, but also scowling to let me know he's not to be messed with. "I'm not trying to rob you for your textbooks."

It's Ever. I rarely see César on the block without Ever at his side. He's backed by three other guys, all of them staring at me intensely.

"I heard you were there yesterday," Ever says. "When they snatched up César."

I nod, my heart pounding. They don't think it was my fault, do they? My abuela didn't raise me to be scared of anybody, but I know better than to think Ever and the Dioses are people you can be casual around. I always have to be careful with them. César may be intimidating, but he's family. Ever is not. I start to sweat.

"I heard it was Moore that made the call," Ever says, his eyes flashing.

"Where'd you hear that?" I ask.

"Lots of places." He shrugs. I think of all the dudes walking past me and César on the way out of school. It never occurred to me that some of them might already be with Dioses del Humo. The paranoid feeling gets stronger and I realize Ever isn't someone I should lie to.

"Yes." I nod. "I'm pretty sure it was Moore."

"Moore has been a problem for years," one of the other guys, Jorgito, says. "He got my uncle locked up too. People like him think they're cops, it's all a power trip."

"Principal, cop, it don't matter," a guy whose name I don't know says. He has a scar on his face, and his eyes look sad. Like César's looked in the back of the cruiser. "We war with anybody."

"Which is why you and me need to talk," Ever says. He fixes me with a stare that roots me to the spot. It's like looking into a snake's eyes. "César said he's talked to you before about joining the Dioses. This could be the perfect time for you. You're on the inside—if something were to happen to Moore . . . maybe that's considered initiation."

My heart freezes. The world suddenly seems very loud. The bus is roaring up to the stop, blowing a cloud of exhaust out over us. We all bat the smoke away from our faces, and when it's gone, Ever is looking straight in my eyes.

"Think about it," Ever says, glancing around to make sure nobody's watching. "We'll give you what you need, just say the word."

We lock eyes. I can almost hear my pulse in my ears, fear and dread drumming in my heart. But still, I'm interested in what he's saying. Anger like a small fire in my stomach, growing. The idea of revenge.

"Catch your bus," Ever says, taking a step back, letting me know I'm dismissed. I finally break his gaze. "Let us know what you decide."

"I'll . . . I'll let you know," I say.

Then I'm on the bus, being carried down the block toward Promise, but when I look out the back window, Ever is still staring after the bus. Something feels different inside me. Like a volcano has started to stir. I don't know how long I can keep it from erupting.

Luis meets me at my locker.

"I tried calling you last night," he says. "I'm so mad about what happened to César. I'm sorry. Are you okay?"

I shake my head. Luis has been my best friend for a long time—he's been busy with basketball lately, and I've kind of been in my own world too, focusing on the future, trying to keep my head down in my neighborhood. But some friends are for life, no matter what happens. And I can tell that even though my whole neighborhood is looking at me sideways, making all their assumptions about me being just like my primo, Luis isn't like that. He knows who I am.

But do I even know who I am? Today I can't seem to shake the feeling I got when Ever told me he would give me what I need to take revenge on Principal Moore. That brief spark that said *Yes* when I imagined holding a gun in my palm, the idea of the dude who got my cousin arrested for no reason, the dude who's always yelling at us, always has us apologizing and stuttering . . . the idea of making *him* apologize for once.

"Whoa, what is all *this*?" Luis exclaims, peeking into my warmer bag.

I shake off all the ugly thoughts of guns and Moore, and manage to smile at my best friend.

"This is César's bail money," I say, trying to sound confident. I've never tried to sell this much before. It's going to be hard, knowing that I just got in trouble last week. But desperate times call for desperate measures, and I can't have César sitting in jail. We were just starting to be honest with each other. And now, I need to be the big cousin for once.

"You're going to need help," Luis says, and I already know what he's thinking. When you've been friends as long as me and Luis have, you just know. He's going to do like he's done before: sell as many pupusas as he can. He's cool with the jocks and I know those guys eat more than anybody in the damn world. He can probably sell them fifty on his own. But I can't let him.

"Nah, Luis," I say, shaking my head. "If anybody sees you doing it, you'll also be screwed."

"Relax," he says. "They're not doing nothing to me with the game today. They know they want my highlights for those donors to see. They'll probably just give me a demerit and mess with my count.

Whatever. I can deal with that. Give me some. And don't forget to go by Ms. García's room—she's, like, the only person who doesn't care that you sell. I bet she'll buy a few."

He's right—Ms. García is always a safe bet. Same with some of the lunch ladies. So, I give him a third of the load, and we split up. It's going to be a stressful day, and carrying this much product around the school really does make me feel like a dealer. *Beep beep beep.* I can already hear the demerits. All those counts rising.

Anyway, this is for César. He wasn't doing anything wrong. Who's to say the cops didn't plant the gun? They do it all the time. And what's so wrong about selling pupusas?

We're not supposed to talk, but we always find a way to communicate. Some guys even have a Promise sign language that they use. Either way, word gets around that I'm raising money for César's bail, and before I know it, the pupusas are flying out of my bag. One kid from around my way buys enough to feed a whole family. I privately wonder if he's a Dioses, but I don't ask. I just slide him the stuff and he slides me the money.

Maybe I'm imagining it, but by noon, the whole school smells like my abuela's secret recipe. And everything is going okay until this guy Victor rips his pants in the cafeteria at the same time Principal Moore is walking through on inspection.

Victor was sitting like everybody else, but when he goes to stand, his belt loop must get caught just right because I hear the *ripppp* two rows over. It rips the belt loop and the pocket, and something falls out onto the floor. I already know what it is, and my stomach turns over, because Moore is passing right in front of him.

He hears the sound, and his head spins with the quickness. I see his eyes laser in on Victor, whose face is shocked. He can't play it off. Moore swoops in.

"What's going on here?" he snaps. "Who's fooling around? I see your face looking like that—you messing around? Disorderly conduct?"

He goes on chewing out Victor, and all the while I'm praying he doesn't notice what's on the floor. But then Moore gets real quiet. I see him looking down, peering over his glasses. Shit.

It's a foil-wrapped pupusa. Moore stares at it for what seems like a long time, and then his eyes sweep over the cafeteria. I know he's looking for me. And when he finds me, he marches over like he's made of lightning.

"Do you think I was playing with you when I told you I didn't want to see this again?" he shouts. "You think our sponsors want to see this shit in our school? This street food garbage? Got this school smelling like a block party. I should have known what you were up to. Where's that bag? I know you've got it."

"I . . . I . . ." But I can't find the words. All the English flies out of my head. The Spanish too. All I feel is anger. It thrums through me.

"And now you're in my face stuttering," he mocks. "I don't know why we've kept you in this school—that ESL isn't working too well, is it? Now give me that . . ."

I can't speak, but when I see him moving to reach under my chair, I rush to stop him, pushing his hand out of the way and snatching at my bag. But he grabs the back of my jacket and pulls me up off the seat, shoving me away. Then he grabs the bag. It still has a bunch of pupusas left and he shakes it, listening.

"Just like I thought."

I go to reach again, my anger soaring, but the guy next to me clutches my arm, anchoring me. I watch as Moore marches over to a trash can, and the whole cafeteria is watching, silent. One by one, he takes the remaining pupusas and throws them into the trash. I want to yell and throw up at the same time. When he's done, he takes a juice bottle from a nearby kid and pours the whole thing in. Then he takes the chunk of money I have from my sales and pockets it. No one says a word.

"This is mine now for selling on school grounds. As for you," he says, pointing straight at me. "You've got detention for the next six weeks. And if you think that senior cooking initiative is going on another day, forget about it."

He turns to the lunch line, where a couple guys who are part of the initiative are watching. I see Lunch Lady Adams scowling like she wants Moore to crumble to dust.

"That's the last day for that, boys," he shouts at the dudes wearing hairnets. "Thank your friend here. Chef Ramón, right? Maybe you'll be a chef in prison one day."

He takes the bag and leaves. When he's gone, people gradually talk quietly again. But not me. All I can think about is the money I won't have now to get César out on bail. The anger sweeps through me, taking control of every part of my body. I need someplace to put it. It's time to do something with it. I walk to the bathroom and take out my phone. I scroll to Ever's number.

PART FOUR

Lies

After the Murder

CHAPTER TEN

Grounded

J.B.

don't think I've ever seen my mom cry in public.

In Benning Terrace you need your game face on at all times, and my mom is a pro at the game face. Always smooth, always about her business. I've always admired that about her. But when I step out of the interrogation, her eyes are a deep red and she hasn't even bothered to wipe her tears. It's gut-wrenching.

"We're releasing your son into your custody," one of the detectives tells her. He makes his voice sound all caring.

"Why wasn't I allowed to be with him?" my mom demands, ignoring his statement. "My son is a minor. I'm supposed to be with him for something like this."

"Ma'am, we're on your son's side. We just want to help."

The lie makes me want to reach for his gun, put it to his temple, and make him apologize. Not for roughing me up when he arrested me, or locking me in the room with the one light and the dark window. Or for yelling in my face, trying to get me to confess to a murder I didn't commit.

I want to make him apologize for lying to my mother. For having the audacity to treat me the way he did, look my mom in the face, and tell her some bullshit.

But I swallow that anger and my stomach starts to boil.

I want to tell my mom the truth, but it'll only make this whole mess worse. So, I stand there silently, trying not to look as scared as I feel.

By the time my mom wraps up the paperwork with the police, it's late, and I can barely keep my eyes open. I nod off, the cool glass of the car window a welcome pillow after being in that interrogation room and holding cell. But the slamming noise of my mom's car door wakes me up with a jolt.

"J.B.," she says quietly, so low I can barely hear her. "If there was ever a time for you to be honest with me, the time is now. I need you to look at me."

I do as I'm told. I lock eyes with my mom, waiting for her to ask me *the* question, but it's too hard for her.

"I didn't do it, Ma," I say softly, helping her out.

She lets out a heavy exhale as if she'd been holding her breath since walking out the police station. "Of course you didn't, baby. Of course you didn't."

A deep relief sweeps over me, knowing that she doesn't think I killed Principal Moore. With everything that happened today—blood still dried under my fingernails—I'm glad she still looks at me and sees an innocent boy. I am innocent.

"I know your relationship with Principal Moore was complicated," she says.

All the anger swirls up again. The feelings I've pushed away since everything went down.

I'd been so angry with Moore. The unfairness of him taking my phone and making me leave Keyana hanging, ruining our relationship.

156

The way he got in my face, grabbed me by the collar like a dog he was punishing, making a fool of me in front of half the damn school. But I never wanted Moore killed. I never wanted him dead. And now, I'm a suspect?!

I've seen enough dudes go to juvie to understand that all the cops need is a motive, a body, and a weapon. They're almost there. They can force people into making confessions and taking pleas just because they're scared.

Punching my locker probably doesn't look great. But the worst part of it all is . . . that gun.

I can't stop thinking about it. The day's events play on a messy, twisted loop. It can't be a coincidence that the same day I found a gun in school, Principal Moore was shot. A gun I moved to keep other people safe, leaving behind my fingerprints! I feel like an idiot.

I have to get that gun back and figure out who owned it before the cops find it—and my fingerprints all over it. That'd be a layup for them. Easy conviction.

I press my fist against my mouth to keep any sound from coming out. I want to cry. My mind is running wild. A terrible future flashes: going to jail, leaving my mom alone, being locked up until she's old. My throat tightens.

My mom turns at the next corner. "J.B., I just don't know what to tell you. I sent you to that school so you could stay out of trouble, but somehow you still find it."

How do I tell her that whether I'm looking for trouble or not, it finds *me*? That being a young Black man makes me a magnet for trouble. All I've done is try to stay under the radar and it's not enough. Especially when there's someone like Moore around, who carries trouble with him like a bucket of paint, ready to throw it all over whoever he wants.

I think of the dude, Solomon, that Moore pounced on for not wearing a tie. Or even the other two kids that are suspects, Ramón and Trey. Word is Moore embarrassed them the day of the shooting too. Hell, there's a hundred dudes at Promise that probably wanted to put a gun to Moore's head.

And that's when it hits me.

Somebody killed Moore, that's a fact. Also a fact? There's a ton of people who probably wanted him dead. I'm an obvious suspect, but what if the person who did it is a not-so-obvious suspect?

The best way to clear my name, maybe the only way, would be to find out who did it. I ball my fists. The clock is ticking. I've got to figure out who did this before people start really trying to stack up the evidence against me.

My mom glances over at me. For a minute, her brows soften. "Are you okay?"

"I'm fine," I say. But it comes out a little too quick, too forced.

"We're going to get through this," she says. It almost sounds like she's talking to herself as much as she's talking to me. "We're going to get through this."

I don't say it out loud, but I think it, hard: *God, I hope so.* Then I think about something else. Keyana.

"Ma, can I use your phone to—"

I'm shocked when she interrupts me with a loud, sarcastic laugh.

"Boy, if you think you're using *any* phone to call *any*body you're out your mind. You may not be a murderer but you are *grounded* as hell, you hear me? Until future notice."

I don't even try to argue. I can't blame her. At least she doesn't think I did it. I can only hope Keyana feels the same way.

At home, Mom seems a lot calmer but I can tell her mind is turning. Not only did she miss out on money by having to come down to the station, she's probably thinking about all the money she's *going* to miss out on with this fiasco. Since it's just the two of us, lost time and money count a lot.

This same thing happened with my pops. Lawyers, fines, court appearances and hearings and shit. All the more reason I need to clear my name. My mom has been carrying enough weight, for enough years. Something like this might break her. I can't let that happen.

She warms up leftover potpie and we share it at the table, eating silently. I make mine disappear—I hadn't realized how hungry I was. But even still, my whole inside feels empty. I have a feeling I could eat the plate too and it wouldn't fill me up. Worry digs at me.

"I just don't know how this happened," she says softly. "I tried my best."

"It's not your fault, Ma," I say back. And I want to add, *It's not my fault either*. But all I can think of is Moore's voice booming down the hall, Hicks and his mean eyes. Demerit after demerit. All those counts rising. All those detentions. Everything is your fault at Promise.

"You didn't hate him, did you?" she asks. She looks straight at me, eyes shining. And this hurts more than anything else, because even though she believes I'm innocent, I can tell she's terrified that she might be wrong.

And the worst part is, I don't know if I can say *no* without it being a lie. Luckily, she goes on talking.

"You wouldn't do something like this. One of those other boys, maybe. I don't know how other people raise their kids. Kids who don't respect authority . . ."

Potpie roils around in my stomach. She doesn't understand. I stare down at my knuckles, still scabbed up from punching the locker. Moore looked at me like I was a criminal for doing that. Was I a criminal? Or was I just human? At Promise, it's almost like showing emotions is another way of breaking the rules.

"What happened to your knuckles, J.B.?"

She's seen me looking, and she stares down at my hand with her eyes big.

"I . . . I . . . got mad," I manage to get out.

"Did you hit someone?"

"No, ma'am," I say.

She stares me deep in my eyes. "Do you promise me?"

"I promise."

But even as I say it, all I hear is the anthem:

> *We promise.*
> *We are the young men of Urban Promise Prep.*
> *We are destined for greatness.*

Its sound haunting in my mind. Am I destined for greatness or for something much worse?

Later on, I'm in my bed, staring up at the ceiling with the lights off. It's like ever since I got home, all my energy has been drained. Suddenly my door cracks open. Mom walks in.

"J.B.? Are you awake?"

"Little bit."

"I called Ross, my supervisor. He said he has some extra hours for me to make up what I lost if I can come in now. I'll be back in the morning."

My heart sinks. Knowing I'll be sitting in the house alone makes me feel even smaller and lonelier than ever.

"Okay," I say.

"Remember, you're grounded."

"Yes, ma'am."

The house had already been quiet, but with her gone it feels like I'm on a different planet now—just totally silent, totally alone.

I wish Keyana was here.

I wonder what rumors she's heard. I wonder if she believes them. She's just down the block—maybe she's looking through that window I jumped out of and wondering what I'm doing. If I'm okay.

Or maybe she's wondering what kind of dude she let kiss her. Regretting it. Thinking she chose the wrong guy . . .

I sit up straight in bed. My mom said I was grounded, but mostly she didn't want me on the computer or the phone that I don't have. And I need to talk to Keyana. Maybe she can tell me about what people on the block are saying, if there are any rumors that can help clear my name.

I don't even think about it after that—I put on my shoes and I'm out the door.

CHAPTER ELEVEN

Suspects

TREY

I never thought I'd say this, but I'm glad my mom is here.

She came down from New York as soon as she heard what happened, and she seems clean—as close to truly clean as I've ever seen her. It's hard seeing her when she's using, but in some ways, it's even harder seeing her clean. Wanting to be with her, but the anxiety that comes with it—always worrying that the rug will be pulled out from under me. But either way, I'm glad she's here, because facing Uncle T alone would have been too much.

He won't put hands on me with her here, I don't think. But it is total lockdown. The doors might as well have bolts on them. Any time I go to the bathroom, he's in the hall staring at me. I go to the kitchen, he's sitting right there like he was waiting. I even looked out my window and he was by the mailbox with his eyes fastened on my room. I ain't going nowhere. And honestly, I prefer it that way. Seems like nothing but trouble outside this house.

And then there's the lawyer. A guy Uncle T served with is camped out in our dining room, constantly talking in low tones, rustling paperwork. He's wearing big clunky shoes that I want to rag on him about, but I know it wouldn't be appropriate.

I never get asked to join these conversations. Mom doesn't say much, just quietly listens. Uncle T sits there with his jaw like a rock, taking in all the information. I haven't asked what they're talking about. I'm afraid of what they'll say. Afraid of what they'll ask and what the answer will be.

So far, the only words my uncle has said to me are: "I told your ass. I told your ass. After everything I've done for you . . ."

He thinks I did it.

He thinks I took his gun and killed Principal Moore.

And the worst part is, maybe I did kill Principal Moore in a way. What if someone took the gun and decided that day was the day? It's my fault the gun was even there. I should've just taken it home and suffered whatever fate Uncle T decided to lay on me. At Promise and at home, there's no room for error. No matter where I go, I am guilty until proven innocent.

Uncle T hasn't asked me about the gun, though there's no way he hasn't noticed it's missing. He's always cleaning it. But the fact that he hasn't brought it up means he thinks I took it on purpose. He might even be trying to protect me. With silence.

"Trey, get out here!" Uncle T shouts from the dining room.

I leap up off my bed. I open my door and every muscle in my body is in battle—part of me wants to hide under my bed like I'm a little kid, running from the boogeyman. Part of me wants to sprint into the dining room and beg them to tell me everything is a big misunderstanding. All I used to do was joke around in serious situations but I can't seem to find the funny in this. It feels like I'll never joke again.

I step into the dining room and all eyes are on me.

"Trey, I'm going to level with you," the lawyer says. He takes off his glasses and stares at me. "This is going to be tough. You don't have an alibi."

I feel like I'm going to choke.

"Did you do this, baby?" my mom whispers. She looks like she hasn't cried yet but she could any second. The sight of her face makes me want to cry too, not just because of this mess, but because of everything that led us here. Everything in the Bronx. Losing her. Coming here. I stare at the floor.

"No," I say.

"The police are trying to put together a narrative of the crime," the lawyer says. He looks sad. "And we don't have much to give them. You were there after school. You were in proximity to the shooting. You threatened the man, and there are witnesses who've attested to that. The only thing they don't have is . . . the weapon."

I can't help but notice Uncle T flinch. The weapon. Uncle T's gun that I hid in the basement of the school, my fingerprints all over it. Uncle T's fingerprints all over it. It's only a matter of time before they find that gun. I need to get it first.

"I wasn't the only one, though," I say in a rush. "Two other dudes were in there. One of them had been fighting earlier that day. I left to go to the bathroom, who knows what they did while I was gone!"

"Well, that's the thing, apparently none of you can account for one another's whereabouts, which adds a layer of complexity," the lawyer says.

"You can't always blame things on somebody else," Uncle T growls. "They're not going to be interested in what somebody else *might* have done."

"I'm not *blaming* nobody," I shout. "I'm saying I didn't do it!"

Uncle T shoves back from the table, the chair screeching. My mom puts her hand on Uncle T's fist and his face softens.

He turns to me. "The three of us need to have more discussions," my uncle says, narrowing his eyes at me. "Go back to your room. We'll call you when we have more questions."

I drift back down the hall and return to my room. I hurl myself on my bed, checking my phone for notifications. Brandon had texted me once or twice, but then abruptly ghosted the conversation. I have a feeling his mom put a stop to that right away. I got released from custody last night and I'm suspended from school until this whole thing is figured out.

I picture Brandon and the other guys sitting in class silently, walking the blue line, clasping their hands behind their backs. I'm so glad I'm not there. Being out of Promise takes a weight off my chest. Only thing is, it's been replaced with a new weight in the form of Principal Moore's body. Out of the frying pan, into the fire.

I scroll through social media, trying to distract myself. But there's no distraction to be found. Without even meaning to, I find little mentions here and there of what went down at Promise.

I understand not liking the dude, but damn—killing him tho?

They arrested all three of them. Must have been in on it together.

Nah, I hear one of them was off by himself. That he set up the dudes in detention to take the fall.

My gut churns as I read the words. Everybody coming to their own conclusions based on almost nothing. Although I guess it's not nothing—three of us were arrested, after all. Of course, people are going to make some shit up. But come on, I saw one dude with the blood on him, J.B.—they have to know it was him and not me! If a dude got murdered and then there was a guy running away with blood on him, I think it's pretty obvious who did it.

I wonder what the teachers think—I wonder if Mrs. Hall heard the news about me being arrested. She was one of my favorite teachers before she left for maternity leave.

The main reason I loved Mrs. Hall? She's the only teacher I've ever seen catch a tone with Principal Moore. All the other teachers, even Dean Hicks, acted scared of Moore. But not Mrs. Hall. She's tiny compared to him, but I saw her get in his face once, yelling at him to *get his head out of his ass and remember why he started this school to begin with*. I remember he just stared at his feet when she said it.

I decide to see if she has social media—I've found a couple other teachers on there before. Teachers always try to keep their stuff low, but even though they're teachers, they're still people. I find Mrs. Hall on social media eventually, with posts going back like ten years. Most of it isn't public, but I do find a photo she was tagged in from two weeks ago, sitting at a bar and toasting somebody wearing a graduation cap.

My eyes catch the drink in Mrs. Hall's hand. It makes me sit up in bed. I'm not an expert or anything, but I'm pretty sure people aren't supposed to drink alcohol when they're pregnant. It doesn't seem like something she would do.

I'm curious now, so I start digging. There isn't a single mention of being pregnant over the past few months.

Could she be lying about being pregnant? But why?

I flop my phone down on the bed, thinking. I don't know why she'd lie. I think about her cussing Principal Moore out that day. Mrs. Hall is such a nice lady—what did he do to make her so mad? Or did she make him mad? Did he *fire* her? I make up my mind to keep digging.

Outside my door, I can hear the low voices of my uncle and my mom and the lawyer. Part of me wants to barge out there and demand that they include me—it's my life, after all. But part of me wants to hide in this room forever.

No matter what, everyone already thinks I'm guilty. But what's new? In this world it feels like I always have *guilty* painted on my back. This time it's just written in blood.

Nobody

Urban Promise Prep Student

Rumor has it that *obvious* doesn't always mean *visible*. Sometimes what's obvious takes a while to see—the person who pulls a trigger doesn't just disappear into the dark. They are right here among us once we decide we're ready to question everything we think we know. They're always closer than you think. Rumor has it that the person who can kill knows you'll look right at them and then keep looking.

Rumor has it that the truth isn't always ready to be told.

CHAPTER TWELVE

The Setup

RAMÓN

I sit at the wooden table in our kitchen with my eyes closed while Abuela gently rolls the smooth egg all over my face and down my neck. It's an ordinary brown egg, but Abuela cleansed it with salt and lemon, and now rolls and rubs it over my skin, performing a limpia for the fourth time this week. I've been home from school for the past four days, and whenever she's done selling pupusas, this is what she wants to do.

She mutters as she goes, her prayers joining the buzz of the kitchen lights. "Padre nuestro que estás en el cielo, santificado sea tu Nombre; venga a nosotros tu Reino . . ."

I keep my eyes closed when the egg reaches my heart. Abuela has special prayers there: praying for the cleanliness of my soul, for the uplifting of my spirit. She prays and prays, and I do too; her out loud and me in my head.

I never wanted this to happen. Never thought it was possible. But here we are.

After she picked me up from the police interrogation, she said nothing. Neither did I. She just cried silently and I stared out the window of the car, trying to find the right words to say. By the time we got home, I realized there were no right words. There was only the ugliness of the day and the days before it, and behind it all the *beep beep beep* of Promise demerits, combined with the crack of the gunshot. I can't get it out of my head. And they're saying I did it.

Abuela's prayers soften and then go silent, and only then do I open my eyes. She's staring down at the egg, like she's afraid of what it absorbed. She reaches for the glass bowl nearby, and with shaking fingers, cracks the egg inside.

We both gasp.

The yellow yolk is flecked with red dots of blood, bright clots. I squeeze my eyes shut, feeling sick.

I wish I could go back. Turn back time. But to where? In order to avoid the incident with Moore that landed me in detention, I would have to never have made the pupusas. And if I never made them, it would be because César wasn't arrested. In order for César to never be arrested, I couldn't be his little cousin. And on and on. How do I unwind my whole life?

Maybe I should have joined the Dioses a long time ago—dropped out of Promise. My abuela would've been so disappointed in me, but not as disappointed as she is right now, seeing blood in the yolk.

She flushes the whole thing, then cleanses the toilet with salt.

"Ramón," she says when she comes back. She sits next to me and presses her hands to my knee. "I know you could not have done this."

"I didn't do this, Abuela, I—"

"You don't need to explain. I know who you are. But this is big trouble. This is bad. Did something else happen? Something with César? Did you tell those Dioses boys something to make them—"

"No," I insist, cutting her off before she could even ask. I can't tell her the truth. I can't tell her what I asked Ever to do on the phone that day after Mr. Moore embarrassed me.

She looks at me sadly.

"You cannot leave this house," she says. "Do you understand me? This is a dangerous time to be away from home. Both the police and people in this neighborhood are weaving together their own stories. You need to stay out of it and keep your head low until everything is sorted. Until you are safe."

I can tell there's a lot she isn't telling me. My abuela, always trying to protect me. With César being as rough as he is, she's always tried to keep me soft. Sometimes trying so hard that it made me mad. I wonder for the first time how it felt to César, always being seen as the rough one. I think about his eyes the moment before all the police rolled up at Promise. He wasn't looking rough then. He was looking like the primo I knew.

"What is it, Abuela?" I say. "What are you hearing?"

She shakes her head. Frustrated as I am, I know there's nothing I can say to convince Abuela to spit out what she's keeping inside.

I reach in my pocket for my brush—my reflex when I need to relax.

But the brush isn't there. That's where it always is. But it's nowhere. Not in my backpack. Not on the table by the door. And then I remember. The police found it somehow at the scene of the crime. I'm not sure how my brush got there, but it feels a lot like a setup. It must have been in my bag when Moore took it.

Abuela sees me looking and makes a *tsk* noise.

"Come watch my novela," she says.

But I can barely keep my eyes open, all the stress draining me of energy. We watch for a while, but then she tells me I should rest. When I get to my room, I get a text from Luis:

Luis: You doing okay?

Ramón: I guess so. What's happening at school?

Luis: Man, it's hard to tell. Everybody has their own theory.

Ramón: It wasn't me, man.

Luis: I know it wasn't you. It had to be that J.B. dude.

Ramón: I don't think so. I think it was Trey.

Luis: It couldn't have been Trey. He would never do that. But J.B., he didn't talk to nobody. It's always the quiet ones, right?

I think about that—"It's always the quiet ones." The whole damn school was quiet. Moore made us that way. Any of us could be the killer when you put it that way.

I get another text before I can write Luis back. It's Magda.

Magda: Are you okay? I wish I could come over. But I'm supposed to be keeping an eye on César after the Dioses bailed him out. He has an ankle bracelet though—it's not like he's going anywhere.

Ramón: I'm just glad he's home. I can't believe this is happening. Any of this.

Magda: You should hear them talking at Mercy!

Ramón: Let me guess—Becca is leading a prayer circle for our souls?

Magda: I mean, literally yes. But I've heard other whispers too.

Ramón: Like what?

Magda: Do you know a guy named Nico that works in the kitchen at Promise?

Ramón: Mr. Martinez . . . maybe?

Magda: Ya, Nico Martinez.

I know the exact guy she means—he's one of the few people in the kitchen I haven't ever talked to. He's quiet and not very approachable, but the thing that stands out the most about him is his Dioses ink.

Ramón: I know the guy. I think he grew up here, he has Humo ink.

Magda: Yep. People are saying it was payback for César.

I drop the phone onto the bed and rub my eyes. Jesus. This is too much to keep track of. I told the guys to stand down. I thought about asking them to do something to Moore, but I didn't. Now I'm finding out they could've done this anyway. If they had an inside guy it would make sense.

Abuela wants me to keep my head down and out of everything, but what if whoever did this is doing the opposite? They're probably walking around in the world like they're innocent, meanwhile I'm here hiding like I'm guilty. Whoever did it, I bet the cops didn't find a piece of their property at the crime scene like they did me. Stupid.

I open up a text to both Luis and Magda.

Ramón: Can we meet up tomorrow? I need help thinking something through.

Magda: Are you sure Abuela will be cool with that?

Ramón: It will be fine. We can do it while she's selling

Luis: Where do you want to meet up?

Magda: And why?

Ramón: I can't just sit around and wait for them to find me guilty.

Luis: Do you have a plan?

Ramón: Kind of. See you tomorrow. 5:30. My house.

Doña Gloria

pray to every saint I know. I light a dozen velas. I should be cutting the cabbage for the curtido, but all I can do is pray.

My grandson is not this person, even as they are ready to paint whole murals with his mug shot. They tell stories about him like he's dead, like the truth is something to be made more interesting, with garish colors.

Years ago, I might have blamed César. I know there are still some who will do so anyway. And many will blame Ramón no matter what—after all, they might remember the old Ramón; the one who was so angry he punched a hole in the wall of our first apartment. Thirteen years old and in a new country, where people frowned when he fumbled with a new language. The frustration turned into rage, and that rage might have burned him if he hadn't started cooking with me—busying his hands, settling his spirit. Now I see the unfairness of the world turning him back to the angry boy I used to know. It fills me with fear, and sadness.

But I am past blame. I am seeking understanding. The last limpia showed me the truth: that the pure good soul of my youngest grandson is being injected with blood, a thousand tiny bleeding wounds, and it's from walking in a world like this, and maybe even in a school like Promise. It wasn't Moore's blood that was in that bowl, it was my grandson's.

Every day we send our children out into the world, they are inflicted with a thousand tiny cuts. And all the limpias in the world can't clean it, because the wound is open.

So now as I think about who did what, and when, and to whom, I think about wounds. Who is most wounded? Who was wounded by this man that is now dead? Who inflicted a thousand tiny cuts? Who shot the bullet that killed him?

Was theirs a wound of pride? The only pride my grandson has ever shown is the pride in making something with his hands that nourishes his fellow people. A heart like that doesn't carry the kind of pride that can lead to taking someone's life.

At least this is what I tell myself.

When I put away the candles, when I get out the masa and queso, I see the mail on the table. All the bills we have to pay, that these pupusas will pay for, that my grandson hopes his dreams will pay for too. And among all the mail are shiny postcards from PROMISE PREP, asking for donations, asking us to RSVP to the annual auction, announcing new sponsorships, money flowing in and out of the school, making it bigger and brighter. Better, they say, for my grandson.

I just want my grandson to be big and bright. I want him to make it out.

CHAPTER THIRTEEN

Traitor

TREY

I'm not supposed to be out of the house—but it's been five days since I've been out of school and locked in the crib. I've given up scrolling through social media; all it does is make me feel worse. I hate how lies spread faster than the truth.

It's like everybody thinks they're the damn cops now: making up scenarios, building out all these elaborate plots of my plans to murder Principal Moore. Why does nobody dedicate that creative energy to, I don't know . . . coming up with theories of how I *didn't* do it? And it sucks even more that I haven't heard from Brandon. I know it's probably because of his mom, but being stuck in the house with bad dreams and Uncle T to keep me company makes everything worse. At least I have Mom, though. For now.

Sometimes I used to just take long walks to clear my mind. I'd give anything to do that right now. And the more I think about it, the less ridiculous it seems. Rocky's ain't far, and I won't even walk nowhere else after that. Just there and back. That plus a cigar will be enough to get my mind right.

I slip out the window before I can talk myself out of it, and sure enough, walking and feeling free helps right away. I keep my hood up just to ward off any quick recognition, and I walk fast, but it still feels good to be out and about. It's getting dark, and that helps too. Maybe it shouldn't. But the shadows feel comforting.

I'm about to pass the dollar store when I hear raised voices. I freeze, at first thinking they're aimed at me. But they're arguing, and even though my mom always tells me to keep my face out of other people's drama, I slow down, taking a sideways glance from under my hood.

I almost trip. It's Mrs. Hall.

And she's arguing with Detective Bo.

My heart jumps, but my instincts take over and I lunge behind a nearby dumpster, their voices echoing out as they walk to their car.

"You don't have any other leads? I'm telling you, none of those boys did this," Mrs. Hall cries.

"You know I have to be very careful with—"

"Bo, this is *me*! You have to talk to me about this! There's too much at stake!"

"You know the rules, Carla! It's looking bad. There are things I have to consider—"

"Asking you to consider is exactly what I'm doing!" she shouts. I chance a peek around the edge of the dumpster and see her small frame waving her arms. She definitely doesn't look pregnant—it's been months. Shouldn't she at least have a *little* belly? Or if she had the baby already, why were there no pictures of them on her social media?

"Carla, Carla," Detective Bo says, lowering his voice. I can still hear him, but barely. "There aren't any other suspects at the moment, but there is an employee at Promise with a criminal record. Nico something. He works in the cafeteria. Maybe I can look into them."

His voice drops away then, and I strain my ears for a few minutes before I take a chance and peek again. I look just in time to see Mrs. Hall hugging him, kissing him on the cheek. Is *he* her husband? How could it be possible that my favorite teacher, the one who always seemed to understand me—understand us—could be married to the kind of guy who would do and say the kind of shit he did during my interrogation? My whole stomach fills up with a sense of dread.

I need to get out of here. If Bo sees me, I'm done for—and I can't stand seeing Mrs. Hall being friendly with that guy. Maybe I don't know who Mrs. Hall even is. Turns out she's a traitor.

I catch the bus home to get there quicker, the desire for a cigar from Rocky's gone. An idea is growing in my head with every second that passes. On social media, people kept talking about how I yelled "I'll kill you" at Moore in the cafeteria. That's why they think I'm the murderer. What a dumbass thing to do. I got written up for it, obviously.

But now after hearing Mrs. Hall and Detective Bo, I'm thinking: Who else has gotten written up by Moore? Who else might have tangled with him? What school employee has a criminal record?

I know all the teachers log into some computer program to track Promise boys' suspensions and demerits and all that. If I could just get in, I could see all that too—and maybe see who else had a problem with Moore the week of the murder.

At home, I pace in my room. Who can get me into the system? Two guys work in the office that I know of—Solomon, and the quiet Dominican guy. I think his name is Omar. There's no way I can ask Solomon—he hates my ass. Can't take my jokes. I guess he doesn't realize that I joke on everybody. It's all in fun. He would report me in a hot second if I asked him for the login, but Omar might be easier to get to. Maybe he'll remember me lending him a belt that time.

But before I start to text Omar, I comb my memory, and I suddenly recall this one time I helped Mrs. Hall with her computer—technology has never been her strong suit. She had her password written on the back of a sticky note on her desk. Maybe I can try to hack in the system myself. What was that pass code?

I try CarlaHall and when that doesn't work, HallCarla. Then I add 123 at the end of both. Nothing. But the numbers jog my memory; there were definitely numbers. Phone number? No! Classroom number!

CarlaHall222

No. Wait.

HallCarla222

And just like that, I'm in.

I try to swallow down my excitement and nervousness. Then I start exploring the database. There's a little bit of a learning curve, but every social media app is more complicated than this. No wonder adults struggle with social media. I go straight to *discipline record*, and just like that I'm scrolling through all of Promise's staff: teachers, janitors, everybody. It's a lot of information, but once I get the hang of it, it's easy to open each file and then scroll down to the same place: records.

Detective Bo was right—there are a couple people with records.

Coach Robinson is one—I knew about him and his background. He'd always talk about his past life, using it to warn me and the guys to stay on the straight and narrow. But I don't blink at him—he was at the game in the gym when the murder happened. Couldn't have been him. Plus he'd never.

But then there's a guy named Mr. Martinez, who works in the cafeteria. I know his face. Marked as a felon in his file. Damn. I can't help but think that could be me. How can I judge him, knowing what I'm up against? But because I don't know anything else about him, I make a mental bookmark of his name and face. I'd hate to point the finger at somebody else, but all I know is that it wasn't me, and I need to prove it.

I switch out of the staff records and into the student body's— looking at anybody who's been written up in the last thirty days. But I don't even need that long. I just need to see the past week.

I see my name, of course. And a bunch of other dudes' names for stuff like uniform violations and talking in class. Little shit. I also see the other expected names: Ramón and J.B. The notes in the database are kind of ridiculous. For J.B. it says *Physical altercation, destruction of school property, recommended expulsion.* For Ramón it says *Possession of contraband, vulgar language, insubordination.* Why does everything sound so . . . extreme? I don't even want to read mine. There are all our names, all of us in detention that terrible day. But there's one other name that shows up on the detention roster:

Solomon.

"Hold up," I whisper. "Hold *up* . . . !"

Solomon: vulgar language, unbecoming conduct. And right there in his file I learn Solomon was supposed to be in detention that day, same as me and J.B. and Ramón. But he definitely wasn't there. So, where the hell was he? I don't know, but I'm going to find out. And I know how.

Keyana Glenn

When J.B. shows up at my window, tossing bottle caps, it's almost like seeing a ghost, even though Moore is the one who died. Everything that's happened feels like being in a bad movie, where no one trusts anyone and the killer keeps changing faces. I hoped J.B. was innocent but it's hard for me to trust people, especially dudes. They will smile in your face and then become someone else as soon as you look away.

But as soon as I see J.B.'s face, I know he's innocent. I look down through the window, and even in the dark I can see his soul shining out through his eyes.

"Can I come up?" he whispers, just loud enough to hear.

I nod, breathless.

Me and J.B. have a lot in common, but one of the main things is that people think they know us based on how we look. He looks intimidating to some people, so that means they automatically cast him as the villain in that bad movie I was talking about. And me? People see me—Black, pretty, smart—and they cast me as someone whose feelings don't matter. Like I'm made of steel and they can do whatever they want to me.

When J.B. climbs into my room, he looks at me, his eyes warm and brown, and I low-key want to melt right into them.

I hug him, and he hugs me back, and we stay locked in each other's arms for a long time before I hear him whisper:

"I need your help." I just nod. But then he pulls back from the hug. "But first, I need to just look at you."

And he does. I'm uncomfortable at first, with him just standing and staring, but the look in his eyes is like one of those special lights they put on plants. I feel myself growing and opening. When he kisses me, I feel like every part of me blooms.

"I missed your face," he says later, when I'm on my bed rubbing his neck. "Your voice too."

"Game," I tease.

"No game," he says seriously. "You're special to me."

I don't even know what to say to that—my heart feels too full. So I just keep rubbing his neck and say, "So what do you need my help with?"

"Clearing my name."

I swallow.

"They're saying there's two other suspects," I manage to say.

"There are. I don't know which one pulled the trigger, but I need to find out."

I light up.

J.B. doesn't know this—nobody does—but I want to be a lawyer. Not the kind that puts people in jail, but the kind that keeps people from going in. A defense attorney. Without even knowing, J.B. asked exactly the right person.

"Of course," I tell him. And I mean it.

Many people don't realize that a lot of what it takes to be a lawyer is detective work. Asking the right questions to the right people at the right time. So, when J.B. leaves my house, I get to work.

I don't go to Promise, obviously, but I know a bunch of girls who have brothers, boyfriends, and cousins at Promise. And girls are the ones who know everything. People act like it's just because of gossip, which is bullshit. Everybody knows dudes are the biggest gossipers in the world so that's not it.

Girls have to notice everything. Especially ones like me. It's a survival mechanism. It's how we keep our heads above water in a world that's so incredibly dangerous for us. We notice everything, take stock of possible threats, and lock it all in our memory.

By the time I get to school the next day, I have a nice list of people I need to talk to. Keisha, who knows Kendall, who dates Bryan, who goes to Promise. Jasmine, whose brother plays ball with Brandon and Trey. Alexis, whose boyfriend got kicked out of Promise for bad grades. Some of the clues feel like dead ends, but some of them are live wires. I take notes on everything I hear. I get phone numbers. I write down dates. All this while still paying attention in class, because I don't play about my grades.

Still, with J.B. not having his phone, there's only one way I can talk to him about everything I've learned.

CHAPTER FOURTEEN

Omar

J.B.

I never thought Keyana was the type to cut school, but there's something special about knowing that she's not just cutting—she's cutting to spend time with me. And after so many days mostly alone, with my mom coming and going, working extra shifts at the hospital, seeing Keyana show up at my door feels like sunshine on my back in January.

She's shy in my house at first, and I make sure we stay in the living room so she doesn't get nervous, or think I'm trying to pressure her into something. I still can't believe she's my girlfriend. I had wondered if she would still want to be after everything that's gone down, but she keeps looking at me with those eyes that say she feels the same way I feel about her.

We sit down on the couch and stare at each other for a minute. Being here side by side feels different. She actually did it—she came to help. She believes me. At least enough to be here.

"I'm glad you came," I say suddenly to break the silence. I fight the urge to kiss her as she stares back at me with those beautiful lips.

"I'm glad I did too," she replies. "I wouldn't just ghost you, you know."

"That's partially why I came over the other night," I say. "I wanted you to know I was thinking about you. That I didn't ghost you. I know that's what you thought for the game. When I . . . you know."

"I mean, I didn't think you ghosted me once the cops showed up," she says, staring down at the carpet. "I did think so before that, though."

"It was Moore," I say angrily. "I would've been there if it wasn't for that maniac."

She purses her lips, and her eyes get big. But they stay on the carpet. "It sounds like y'all had beef," she says softly.

I grit my teeth. "This is why this whole thing is so fucked up. Because we did. After that day, what he did . . . I hated him. But I wouldn't kill anyone. That's why I came to your house. Because I can't do this alone. I need somebody to believe me."

She's quiet, and my heart clenches up.

"You do believe me, right?"

"Yes," she says slowly. "But I do have questions."

"I know," I say. "So do I. But I think I know how to find the answers. Somebody brought a gun to school that day. I need to figure out who."

Keyana's eyes get big. "What! How do you know?"

"I found it in the bathroom in the basement of the school."

Keyana leaps out of her seat. "Did you tell someone at the school when you found it?"

"No."

"Why not?"

"So people could think I was a snitch? That's a death sentence. And I definitely can't tell the cops at this point."

Keyana cocks her head to the side. "Why?"

I go quiet. "I was scared someone was going to use it, so I moved the gun. I put my fingerprints on it."

Keyana goes quiet for a long time. I think she's going to get up and leave, but she doesn't budge. "Where you'd move it to?" she asks in a low voice.

"A ceiling panel in the basement."

"We need to go check on that gun, but give it some time. The cops are probably watching the place."

"Okay, what about in the meantime?" I ask.

"Well, I was thinking about what you said the other night," she says, focused. She leans into the couch. "And I started asking around. Because we really need to figure out exactly who did this. Not just to clear your name, but also so the cops can't just use it as an excuse to keep harassing every Black or brown dude that crosses their path."

This is why I like Keyana—because she's so damn smart.

"Asking around . . . where?" I say.

"Everywhere. Like this girl Rachel that goes to my school. Her brother goes to Promise and she definitely thinks that dude Ramón did it. You know him?"

I just shrug. "I don't know the dude. All I know is he be making pupusas and they're good as hell."

A thought hits me.

"Hold up. I did see him headed into the bathroom where the gun was. I don't think he would've found it, but it's possible."

"Of course it is. Rachel said he's on some gang shit maybe. I don't know. What does your instinct tell you?"

I look Keyana in the eyes. "Trey."

"Yeah?"

She reaches in her purse and pulls out her phone.

"Everybody has a theory, as you've probably guessed. But some people have more information than others. Stuff they saw and heard. So, I started making a list, and taking little notes. And out of everyone, Trey seems the most likely."

"Can I see?"

She hands me her phone and I stare down at the notes she's been taking. She did all this in just the couple of days since I went to her window. It's amazing.

LIST OF SUSPECTS

Trey: Wasn't in detention when he was supposed to be. Other students witnessed him threatening Moore earlier that day, said he would kill him.

Ramón: Moore called the cops on his cousin the day before Moore was murdered. Rumors that Ramón was talking to Dioses del Humo that same day.

Omar: Weird kid, the last person seen with Moore.

I look up from the list.

"Omar?!" I say, raising my voice. "Who said *that*?"

Keyana squints, trying to remember. "I'm pretty sure I heard that from a girl whose brother works in the office at Promise. A guy named Sal? Solomon?"

"Solomon," I say, surprised. "I know that guy. He thinks Omar killed Principal Moore?!"

"No, his sister says he definitely thinks Trey did it, but she did say Omar was the last person he saw with Moore. I wrote it down just in case. I think the more suspects, the better."

It was weird to me that I hadn't heard about Omar and Moore. Omar was a quiet kid, which has its advantages in times like these. I'm sure nobody at Promise would ever consider Omar as the murderer.

"I gotta hear more about this. I could text Solomon," I offer. Then my hopes sink. "Damn, I don't have my phone though. I don't even have his number."

"I could text his sister. But do you know his social handle or anything? That might be faster."

I sit up straight again. "Yeah, he's on there. You going to message him?"

She's already on it. I don't even have to tell her his @ . . . she types in *Solomon Bekele* and there he is, already popping up. She sends him a quick message:

I'm trying to prove J.B. is innocent. He says y'all were cool. Can you help?

"Okay," she says. "Now while we wait, let's look at the other suspects."

We sit closer, shoulder to shoulder, looking at the list on her phone. I know I'm supposed to be focused on the case, but she smells so good. It makes me want to close my eyes and just breathe.

Apparently she feels the same way. She leans into me a little, turns her face in my direction. It seems ridiculous to even think about anything else when I'm facing a murder charge, but Keyana is special.

"Wait," Keyana says, excited, jerking away. "Solomon wrote back!"

I'm almost disappointed. But I get my head right. This is important.

Keyana taps on the message quickly.

I'm down to help. J.B. is cool. What can I do?

She grins. Damn, I am lucky to have her on my side.

She types: *I heard you work in the office? Did you see anything?*

We wait impatiently for his reply to pop up.

Hold on, I have to be low. Omar works in here too and I don't want him to see.

"What do you know about this Omar?"

"Real quiet. I've seen him filming stuff for the school before."

A message from Solomon pops up.

"Oh shit, look," Keyana says, delighted.

Solomon has sent two pictures—the visitors' log for the office the day of the murder. It isn't very long, but there's still quite a few names to scroll through.

"Recognize anyone?" she says, frowning in concentration.

I scan the long list, skipping over ones that seem like parents since I recognize the last names.

Then my eye catches on a name I do recognize.

"Mrs. Hall. She's my favorite teacher, but she's been out this year," I say. I think about seeing her buy wine at Mariano's, but there's no way she could've killed someone. "I saw her the day before the murder and she told me she'd met with Moore that day. She seemed pretty upset. Weird she'd come back the next day, but maybe she wanted to continue the conversation?"

"Interesting. That sounds fishy. Let's not dismiss her yet, but is there anyone else on here who you think might be more of a viable suspect?"

"Stanley Ennis," I say.

"Who's that?"

"He's a rich guy." I frown. "He's always coming to games. Apparently he donates money to Promise. He likes getting his name engraved on stuff. One of those guys that really loves feeling like he's a savior. He always seemed nice, but he made me feel weird, you know? Like the kind of white guy that has to puff out his chest extra when he's around Black guys. Even kids. He and Moore would butt heads a lot. But I don't know. I didn't play sports at Promise, and he was all about them."

"Does Solomon play sports?" she says, getting ready to type.

"Not that I know of."

"Do you know anybody we could talk to?"

I pause, thinking. Then it dawns on me.

"You're not going to like this."

"What?"

"Trey. He'd know Ennis."

"Trey?! The guy that a lot of people think *really* did it? The guy who I think did it?"

"I know, I know, but maybe we make sure Trey didn't do this and then ask about Ennis."

She stares at me, looking doubtful.

"You said we gotta consider all leads, right?" I say, nudging her.

"Yeah . . ." She sighs.

"Well, let's hit him up."

CHAPTER FIFTEEN

Angels

TREY

Sneaking out again doubles my risk—but Uncle T's running errands and it has to be done. I haven't thought of anything else since I logged into Mrs. Hall's school database account. I need to talk to Solomon.

Sometimes me and some guys from the team play ball down at Turkey Thicket Rec Center. It's one of the few places in the city with an indoor court. I almost always see Solomon there playing soccer, so that's where I start.

Luckily for him, I'm not there for beef—but if I had been he'd be in some shit. Instead, when I get to the park, I stand there on the sideline, scanning the field while trying not to be seen.

Too late.

The same time I spot Solomon, his friends spot me. One or two of them go to Promise and I see them get nervous. They nudge Solomon, and when he notices me, he freezes.

"Man, come here, I just need to talk to you!" I call.

He doesn't move at first.

"You're wasting my time, man, ain't nobody trying to do nothing to you."

He wanders over against his better judgment, afraid to look like a punk.

"What's up?"

"Where were you that day, man?" I try not to sound like a cop. But I really need to know.

"When?"

"The day he died. The day Moore died. You were supposed to be in detention with us. But it was just me, J.B, and Ramón. So where were *you*?"

Solomon glances over his shoulder and takes a step toward me.

"How did you even know about that?" he says, eyeing me. "And why do you care?"

"Why do *I* care? What you mean, why do I care? Because I'm a suspect in this murder, that's why! And if it wasn't me—which it *wasn't*—then I need to figure out who it was before I get jammed up." I stare him down. "I'm thinking maybe it was *you*."

He looks at me with this face that tells me that until this moment, he thought I did it. Probably just because he's being petty about me roasting him, 'cause he doesn't know the real me. Anybody who did would know I was innocent.

"Just because I wasn't in detention doesn't mean I did it, what the hell!" he says.

"Well, where were you, then? Do you even have an alibi?"

"I don't have to tell you nothing, I—"

"Man, if you don't just tell me . . . ! You don't have nothing to hide, right?"

"Dean Hicks said I could sort papers in his office," he snaps. "I told him I wasn't comfortable being in detention with you, so he said I could serve it in his office. Okay?! Happy now?"

I stare at him, suddenly feeling guilty. I thought he knew it was just jokes. But it turns out I made this kid feel like he couldn't even be in the same room with me. That's a shitty feeling. But I need to focus on the matter at hand.

"Okay," I say. "You were in his office. So he's your alibi."

"Yeah. He was in there with me until he got a text from security saying to check on a situation, so he left. But I was logging all kinds of stuff in the computer and there's time stamps for all of that. You can probably figure that out if you figured out I was supposed to be in detention."

He stares at me like he wants to fight, but I know he doesn't.

"I had to ask, man," I snap. It's not like I was hoping he did it or anything, but I was hoping he would be able to offer *something* that would take the heat off me. "At least I asked! I know you out here spreading all kinds of rumors. I saw your post on the 'gram—talking about the basketball team playing games in jail. You think that shit is funny?"

He looks embarrassed but mad, and fires back: "You're wasting your time anyway! If you were smart, you'd be talking to that dude Ramón—yeah, I thought you did it at first, but then I heard they found something of Ramón's at the crime scene. You need to be talking to *him*. Or, hell, Omar. I saw him leaving Moore's office that day. I told the other kid that too, J.B. Don't come at me like I did something—I didn't."

Then he turns around and goes back to his soccer buddies, all of them glaring at me as I walk off the field.

What a damn mess. I never even thought that Ramón kid was a real possibility. Dude always seemed chill. But who knows what happened when I left detention that day. And Omar?! That doesn't even seem possible.

I make my way back home, feeling even worse than when I left. As

I climb back in through my window, I'm shocked to find my room isn't empty. I trip and fall headfirst onto the floor.

My mom is sitting on my bed with her hands in her lap.

"Ma! Dang! You scared the hell outta me!"

"Watch your mouth," she says gently, but she barely means it. She studies me, and her eyes look tired and sad. "How are you holding up?"

She doesn't even ask me where I've been, doesn't say anything about me breaking Uncle T's rules.

"I don't even know, Ma," I say. I can barely look at her. I flop down on the bed and cover my eyes with one arm.

"Pick two feelings," she says.

My heart clenches. She used to do this when I got upset when we still lived together. As a little kid, I would hyperventilate, couldn't even breathe. As I got older, instead of hyperventilating, I would just shut down. Silent as a stone. Feeling nothing. But hearing her say those three words makes my breath speed up.

"Pick two," she repeats softly.

I try to zero in on what's happening inside me. It's so hard when everything is a storm.

"Fear," I whisper. "And disappointment."

"I understand fear," she says. "What are you disappointed about?"

"It feels like . . . like everything is slipping away. All my hopes and dreams. The one thing I'm good at slipping away. That game could've changed everything. I guess it did in a way—the worst way. All because of that dude."

"What else?" she says. Even when she was having a hard time, she could always press me a little further. She could always tell when I was holding back.

"And I guess . . . I guess . . . I guess I'm disappointed in . . . Uncle T.

In Brandon, my best friend. In Mrs. Hall. All these people that are supposed to have my back and they just . . . don't."

"Me too."

"Huh?"

"And me too. I'm supposed to have your back. And I haven't."

"It's not your fault, Ma," I mumble around my arm. "You're dealing with your own stuff."

"You *are* my own stuff," she says. "Look at me, Trey."

It takes me awhile to get up the courage to move my arm, but when I do she's shifted a little closer. When I meet her eyes, she smiles a sad smile.

"I'm sorry this is happening," she says. "I wish I could change so many things."

"It is what it is," I mutter.

"No, it's not," she says, and surprises me when her voice grows louder. Since she's been here at Uncle T's, she's been so quiet and meek. "We're not going to take this lying down, okay?"

"Tell that to Uncle T," I say. "He's probably just waiting for the guilty verdict."

"When he left earlier? He was headed to a meeting to talk to another lawyer," she says softly. "Somebody who doesn't already believe you're guilty. And remember, you haven't been charged with anything yet. We're going to keep praying and keep making friends. I'm following the angels on this and you should too."

I don't say it out loud, but I think, *What angels are looking out for me? All I got are people making me out to be the devil.*

"I think your phone is going off," she says, shifting. She pulls my phone out from under her leg and passes it to me.

"Yeah, it's been going off all day," I say as I check my messages. "Everybody has been hitting me up about this Moore situation."

When I get to the bottom of my messages, I see one from an account I don't follow. Some girl named Keyana.

We're trying to figure out who really did this, the message says. *Are you in? Meet us at Meridian in an hour.*

I stare at the message, eyes wide. I click on Keyana's profile and she has a FREE J.B. post on her page. Just who I was needing to speak with since I now know from Solomon that he's also going around asking questions. My mom peeks over my shoulder.

"Angels, like I said," she whispers.

"Uncle T said I can't leave the house," I say, still staring at the message. Like I'm looking for an excuse. But then I hesitate: What if it's a setup?

"Well, you already broke the rules once," she says with a tiny grin. "We'll go together. Your uncle can blame me if he wants."

"It might be dangerous, Ma."

She narrows her eyes. "Boy, who's your mother? Put your shoes on."

CHAPTER SIXTEEN

Handoff

RAMÓN

I'm supposed to be meeting Magda and Luis soon, but I have something else I need to do first. I didn't tell Magda because I know she would be mad, but there's a feeling building in me that's like the sparks before a wildfire. A bunch of small blazes growing into a big one. And it's been growing more and more. Anger, fear, resentment. I try to swallow it all down. But I'm running out of space.

Ever is walking just ahead of me. I've been following him out of our neighborhood. I can't get my mind off the day of the murder. I went to the bathroom in anger and called Ever. I told him I wouldn't have the money for my primo's bail because of what Moore did. He told me not to worry about it. He said the gang would cover it and Moore would get what he deserved.

What did he mean by that? I had to find out.

Ever turns a corner and I hang back a few feet. From behind a bush, I glance at the address he walks up to: 314 Bosetti. I write it down in my phone.

Once he's at the door with his back to me, I start inching closer. I don't know what I'm looking for. What if he sees me? Would he hurt me? Even try to kill me? But my instincts tell me he's the best place to start looking for answers, so I chose to tail him.

My heart pounds as I think about facing Ever. I look around at the faces on the street, careful to make sure no other Dioses spot me. If word gets back I was following Ever, it could look suspicious.

As I approach the building, I see a guy come out to meet Ever. He's full of tattoos. Especially Dioses ink. They turn to look down the street and I duck behind a tree. I close my eyes as if that'll make me more invisible. And even though this is far from a game, it reminds me of the hide-and-seek games César and I use to play.

I peek from behind the tree to try to get a look at Ever, and what I see makes me start sweating buckets.

Mr. Martinez.

Mr. Martinez, or Nico as he told us to call him, was a younger guy who worked in the kitchen at Promise. He couldn't be much older than César. He is one of the few El Salvadoran staff members at Promise, so we always had a connection. Nico was quiet. Serious eyes, serious face. Sure he was intimidating, but I thought he might've put the Dios life behind him years ago. But maybe not?

I need to get a better look, but it's risky. I try to walk as close to the storefronts as I can in case I need to jump in one to avoid Ever's gaze. But then they start walking around the building to the alley next door. I follow them, peeking from around the corner.

Ever takes out a bulging envelope from his jean pocket and slips it to Mr. Martinez. I've seen exchanges like this before and have no doubt the envelope is packed with cash. Nico takes the money and walks through the back door into the building. Ever starts walking back this way and I take off, hiding behind another tree.

That was odd.

I watch Ever head down to the intersection, where he turns a corner and disappears from my sight. When he's gone, I walk back to the building 314 Bosetti. When I get there, I see it's an El Salvadoran restaurant called El Rincón.

My throat tightens up, all the fire spreading through my chest. I think about my abuela and what it would feel like being away from her if I go to prison—all because somebody killed a man I hated and let me take the fall. For all I know, it could have been Nico Martinez. He has opportunity, motive. And now receiving some sort of payoff from Ever? This felt like a solid lead, but I need to learn more before I tell Magda and Luis.

Change of Plans

Magda, Ramón, Luis

Magda: Still meeting at 5:30?

Ramón: Yep, and I have some info.

Luis: I'll be there. What info?

Ramón: Prefer not to text it.

Luis: Jason Bourne shit, I love it. We're coming to your house, right, Ramón?

Ramón: I was actually thinking we should meet at the park. The Dioses have been hovering around a lot. I don't want them even near us when we talk. The last thing I need is you two getting in some mess.

Magda: Valid. What should I tell César?

Ramón: Nothing yet. I'm going to talk to him on my own. I just don't know what to say yet.

Luis: Which park?

Ramón: Meridian

Luis: Cool, see you then.

Magda: . . . . you're bringing pupusas right?

Ramón: of course

Luis: BOOST!

CONGRESSWOMAN
FORD'S BRIEFING

Rarely do we see a case that affects so many facets of our community. A hero to many, a dedicated servant to those among us who most need a helping hand, the loss of Principal Kenneth Moore is one that reverberates throughout this city, and we will be tireless in calling for justice.

This case is continuing to develop, and I will be keeping a close eye on how it proceeds. Dean Wilson Hicks has reported that there is unfortunately nothing to be found on the school's security footage, but I am hearing that incriminating emails from an anonymous sender will be made public today, which may help guide the course of this investigation. The hope is that someone will recognize something in these emails—information; a way of speaking—to aid police in finding the killer.

In light of this, on the screen you'll see the number for a tip line that can be called if anyone recognizes any information in the emails when they're released. In the meantime, I will be working closely with other lawmakers, in partnership with the school board, to develop new legislation about school resource officers, whose presence may prevent this kind of terrible event in the future.

Good Night, Primo

Ramón: Primo

César: ?

Ramón: I don't want to go to jail.

César: . . .

Ramón: You have nothing to say? Do I make you ashamed?

César: How could I be ashamed of you?

Ramón: No sé

César: How?

Ramón: Did Ever tell you?

César: ?

Ramón: What I told him to do. Or not to.

César: Yea, I heard

Ramón: I'm sorry. I'm not like y'all.

César: I never wanted this life for you. Only your safety.

Ramón: You mean you didn't want Moore dead?

César: I didn't say that. Good night, primo

CHAPTER SEVENTEEN

Trust

RAMÓN

I sit under the gazebo at the center of the park, waiting for Magda and Luis. We used to come here when we were younger. It was out of the Dioses territory, as well as other gangs', so it was a safe place to just hang out and mess around.

Still, I can't help but look over my shoulder every few seconds, like Ever or Nico might be pulling up on me at any moment.

I feel like crap sitting in this park when I'm supposed to be staying in the house. I can only imagine how disappointed Abuela would be if she found out I was sneaking around. But I can't just wait for them to find me guilty.

The park is empty except for me and the shapes of a guy and a girl making their way toward me across the grass. Luis and Magda coming to help me out, just like they said they would.

But as they get closer, I see it's not Luis and Magda. The girl is too short and the guy is too tall. *Way* too tall.

Púchica. It *is* him. J.B. Williamson. I don't know the girl, but she's already seen me and nudges J.B., pointing to another gazebo. He's about to follow her, but then he sees me and freezes. At the same moment, another person appears from the other side of the park, hands stuffed in his pockets and headed this way. Is that . . . ?

I don't even notice Magda come up on me. "Hey, sorry we're a little late." She plops down beside me on the gazebo bench, sipping on a to-go cup of horchata. "I blame Luis."

"That's interesting because I blame you."

They go on bantering, but my eyes are fixed on the figures across the park.

"Magda," I say, but they don't hear me.

"The same way you blame me for Reina not wanting to go out with you?" Magda says.

"That *was* your fault, Magda! I told you to tell her I thought she was cute—not that I wanted to marry her!"

"I remember you literally saying that, though."

"¿¡Callense!?" I snap, slapping at their shoulders. "Look. Are you seeing what I'm seeing?"

Finally, they both look, where no more than a hundred yards away, J.B. Williamson stands with the girl, and fifty yards to their east stands . . .

"That's Trey," Luis says, sitting straight up on the bench.

"Luis, did you tell them to meet you up here?!" Magda cries, pushing his shoulder.

"No! Hell no, that would be weird! I didn't say anything to anybody."

We watch from the gazebo as J.B. and the girl walk slowly over to meet Trey. They stand some distance apart, exchanging a few words. Then they all look in our direction.

"We should leave," Magda says softly. "What are the odds that all three of you are here at the same time? Feels like a setup."

"Nah, this has to be a sign," Luis says.

"A sign of what?" I say, low. "That if someone sees us, people will call it a conspiracy? That we really did plan to kill Moore together?!"

"That's a good point," Luis says. "Maybe Magda's right, we should leave."

"Just give me a second," I snap again.

Magda and Luis go quiet so I can think. I watch the others, watching us, and I get the feeling they're having the same conversation we are.

Before I can decide what to do, I notice Trey looking in our direction, lifting his head in acknowledgment.

"Wussup, Luis," he yells out. "You good?"

Luis pauses, glancing at me, then Magda. "Yeah, I'm good. You good?"

Trey nods, then he and J.B. exchange words. My heart starts to pound as the three of them—J.B., Trey, and the girl—move in our direction. I suddenly regret coming out here.

"Ramón, right?" says J.B. when he walks up. The girl with him is super pretty, brown skin and dark hair. Her eyes are serious. She keeps glancing at Trey, who keeps looking over his shoulder.

"Right," I say, then swallow. "What are you guys doing here?"

Neither of the guys really talks, just kinda mutter. The girl speaks up.

"'Sup, I'm Keyana," she says. "I'm J.B.'s girlfriend." She seems a little shy when she says it, like she's still getting used to it. "We, um, we decided to meet up with Trey so we can figure out what's going on. Because right now it's not looking good for nobody."

"Including you, right?" Trey says, shooting a glance at me. Then he looks over his shoulder again. I don't see anybody except for a lone woman sitting on a bench across the park.

"Is this a good idea?" Luis interrupts. "I mean, some people are saying the three of you planned it."

"All lies and rumors," Trey snaps. "I don't even know y'all."

"*I* know you," Luis says. "You're my teammate, man. I never thought you did it."

"And seems like Ramón is your boy," J.B. says gruffly. "So that means . . . what? That you think *I* did it, right?"

We all glare at each other for a second. The tension is so thick it feels like fog. Luis's face is growing red with anger, but before he can respond, I cut in.

"That's not even the point right now," I speak up. "Right now, we need to make sure nobody sees us."

"There's just one lady over there," Luis says, pointing at the woman I had seen.

Trey mutters something.

"Huh?"

"That's my mom," he says. "She came with me."

Nobody says anything. It doesn't escape my notice that both me and J.B. had someone our age show up for us, but Trey didn't. He must be feeling really lonely.

"So, let's figure this out," Magda says, and Keyana nods. "What do we know?"

"We know I didn't do it," Trey says quickly.

"I *don't* know that," I say.

J.B. turns to me and says, "And I don't know it wasn't *you*. You left detention to make a phone call and then all of a sudden Moore is shot."

He's right. But I had to call back Ever before it was too late. I can feel Magda's eyes on me.

"Well, you're definitely a bigger suspect than me—his blood was all over you!" I snap back.

"That wasn't his blood!" he shouts as he takes a step toward me.

I tense up, expecting him to want to fight. With his size, not sure

I could take him, but I couldn't back down. Keyana jumps in front of him, and I can't say I don't appreciate it.

"This is what we know," she says. "Trey was looking into this thing just like we were. And he found a credible lead. We did too, the same person. So we trust each other. It's you we don't know about. Word is Dioses del Humo could've been involved, not to mention your brush being at the scene."

I gulp.

"How'd you know about that?" I asked.

"Word travels."

"I don't know how it got there, but Moore took my pupusas earlier that day. He had my whole bag!"

"Uh-huh, whatever," Trey says hotly. "Sounds sus to *me*."

The sudden fear makes my anger flare. "And *I* heard they have footage of you sneaking into the school."

He scowls and so do I.

"Isn't your cousin a banger?" he says. "I heard y'all put a hit out."

"Just because my cousin bangs doesn't mean I do," I snarl.

"Rumors and rumors," Magda says loudly to clear the air.

"Well, I didn't do this," I say, needing them to believe me.

"Then who did?" J.B. says, looking more tired than angry.

I can tell J.B. and Trey want to solve this thing as bad as I do. Maybe they really didn't do this and I should work with them. And even if they did, working with them would mean I could keep a close eye on them while looking into other potential suspects.

But I can't tell them about Nico. They'd be too suspicious of me since he's possibly a Dios, or at least was once.

"Y'all, look!" Keyana shouts. "They just released emails from the killer!"

Keyana taps on her phone, and we all lean in to read.

EMAILS RETRIEVED FROM PRINCIPAL MOORE'S DESKTOP

Sender: darkgamble@anonmail.com
To: Principal Kenneth Moore

I know what you did. You were supposed to be there for me, and you decided to turn your back. Don't think I'll forget this. Time is running out for you.

Sender: darkgamble@anonmail.com
To: Principal Kenneth Moore

You ignored my last message, so I will make myself a little clearer. If you don't right this wrong, the blowback will be fast and furious. You think you're immune to consequences? You think those are for everyone else? You're wrong. I know what you did, and you're going to get what's coming. I PROMISE.

CHAPTER EIGHTEEN

Coconspirators

TREY

D amn," says the girl with Ramón. "These are serious."

I like how she frowns, but not because she's mad—because she's thinking. I do that too. So does my mom. I bet she's sitting on that park bench frowning right now, wondering if this was a good idea, just like I am.

"What's your name again?" I ask her.

"Magda." She smiles back. But before I can say anything else, Ramón chimes in.

"Those emails could be from anybody."

"Anybody that goes to Promise, you mean," says J.B. "See how they said *I promise* at the end?"

"Not necessarily *goes* to Promise. Maybe worked there. Or even a parent. Had to be lots of people who beefed with Moore," Ramón says.

"You mean like Stanley Ennis?" J.B. says "Keyana and I got ahold of the visitors' log at school and turns out he was the last person to visit Moore's office the day of the murder."

"Oh yeah," Luis jumps in. "I don't know him well, but he got us new basketball jerseys."

"J.B. says he and Moore would butt heads?" Keyana says, reading the notes from her phone.

I know Ennis. He recruited me for basketball. He even gave Uncle T a nice-sized check for taking me in. He is definitely an interesting guy, always making sure you knew how much money he had. I don't see him killing Moore, but at this point nobody could be trusted. Not even the other boys in the park with me.

"Yeah, I know him," I add. "He and Moore got in an argument once in the back of the gym during practice, 'With all the money I bring in to this school, you need to do what I tell you to do.' You can guess what Moore thought about that. Which honestly, fuck Moore, but I was rooting for him that day, because Ennis is such an asshole. The type to want his name put up on a wall or a bench."

"I remember that," Luis says eagerly. "It was like a month ago. Coach had to ask them to step out the gym. Ennis acted like he owned the place."

"He kind of does," J.B. says. "That Promise Fund shit? We found this article on how he's bringing in all the money to Promise. When money gets involved things get sticky."

I don't think I've ever heard J.B. talk this much. Ramón either. That's the way Promise works: You're side by side with strangers. Until I get to know them better I can't get too close. They could be in on Principal's Moore murder together.

"Oh shit, that makes me remember something else," Luis cuts in. "This was later that day, when I was walking out with Omar. Ennis was in the hall on his phone, and then he shut up when he saw us. But before he did, I heard him say, 'I'm not going to give him another dime if he doesn't come up with some answers.'"

"If anything, Ennis saying he's not going to give Promise another dime sounds like motive for *Moore* to kill *Ennis*, not the other way around," Ramón says.

"Wait, who's Omar again?" Keyana says glancing at me and J.B.

"Oh, he works in the office," Luis says. "Ennis uses him for sizzle reel footage sometimes. He's pretty quiet, don't talk to nobody."

"Except you, apparently," says Magda, and I smile at that. She's quick.

"We were only talking that day because I wanted to make sure he got my dunk on tape." Luis shrugs. "You know I fly."

"Y'all focus," Keyana says. "We heard about Omar. Apparently he was the last person seen with Moore."

"Omar?" Luis scoffs. "No fucking way."

"We just don't know what his motive could be," Keyana says, frowning.

"I've seen the dude and I don't think he did this. But if nobody else is looking at him, then we need to."

"Facts," says J.B. "So, what about somebody like Hicks? He found the body, right? Or even . . ."

"Mrs. Hall," I blurt out before I even know what I'm saying. As much as it makes me feel like shit to consider she could've killed someone, I can't deny she was acting all suspicious.

Both J.B. and Ramón look at me confused.

"I saw a photo of her on social with wine," I say quickly. "I think she might be lying about being pregnant."

J.B.'s eyes widen. "And . . . I ran into her at Mariano's after school the day before Moore was shot and she was buying wine."

"Why would she lie about being pregnant?" Ramón says, surprised.

"I don't know," says J.B. "But when I saw her at Mariano's, she told me she had a meeting with Moore that day."

"Not only that," Keyana says, "she came back to Promise the next day. Her name was also on the visitors' log. But she signed out an hour before the game."

"I don't know her," says Magda, "but if she had something against Moore and wanted to kill him, it would've been smart for her to be seen leaving the school before the murder so she wouldn't be a suspect."

I shake my head. I don't want to believe that. But I keep thinking of seeing her with Detective Bo. I don't know if I should tell the others about what I saw, especially if they're somehow involved. But if they aren't, knowing Detective Bo and Mrs. Hall are connected could be valuable information. This is all so confusing.

"There's something else," I say, hating that we're considering Mrs. Hall. "I, uh . . . I saw her arguing with Detective Bo. And she, uh, she kissed him. I'm pretty sure that's her husband."

"She's married to a *cop*?" Ramón exclaims.

"No way," J.B. says, shaking his head. "Not just any cop, the cop on this case? What the fuck?!"

"Or at least boyfriend," I add.

Magda lets out a little gasp and then says, "¡Qué barbaridad!"

"I know, I saw them," I say. "I heard them talking. She was asking him about suspects. What if she was trying to find out what they might have on her or something?"

"That would be wild," J.B. mutters. "One of the emails had the line, '*You were supposed to be there for me.*' That could be Mrs. Hall, to be honest. Like, if it's not one of us—not a student—then it sounds most like a teacher."

"Damn," Ramón says, nodding, turning it all over in his head. "That actually makes sense."

We all sit in silence and finally I remember the other name on my brain.

"OH! I overheard something else Detective Bo mentioned. A cafeteria guy at Promise who has a criminal record. Nico Martinez."

Right as I say Nico's name, I notice Ramón look at his feet. Uncle T was always watching my body language and using it against me. I'm not sure what looking down meant for Ramón in that moment, but I clock it all the same.

"Does this Nico have any type of motive?" Keyana asks.

"Not that I can tell, but we'd have to do some digging."

"I can do it!" Ramón volunteers. "I think I know who you're talking about. I've seen him around the Heights."

"Cool, well if we're divvying up suspects, we need to recap. Who are we really looking at?"

Keyana consults her notes.

"Well, Mrs. Hall is still on the list," she says, sounding apologetic. "Like, it would be ridiculous for the wife of a cop to commit murder, but maybe she figured he would cover for her? Wouldn't be the first dirty cop."

"Mrs. Hall doesn't live far from me; I'll see what I can find," I say.

"I don't know where Omar lives, but we'll start with him," J.B. says, looking at Keyana.

"Cool," Keyana continues, "and Ennis is still a suspect, even though it's iffy. He donated a lot of money and you know how people are about money. Let's start with Mrs. Hall, Omar, and Nico, and keep the others on the back burner."

"Makes sense to me," Ramón says.

"Me too," J.B. chimes in.

They look at me, waiting for me to agree, but deep down I still don't know if I can trust them.

"Cool," I say.

We all stand there, silent for a second, thinking of our next move.

"Meanwhile," J.B. says quietly after a while. "Life at Promise just goes on. They ruin all three of our lives and it doesn't matter."

Truth. I nod. "I hope they put somebody in charge who's better than Moore."

"I'm sure it'll be Hicks," Ramón says.

"Don't matter who they put in that spot, they'll always question our character. Young and Black? They hate us in America," J.B. says, and I can tell by the way he says it he's almost quoting a song.

"Cordae?" I say. We lock eyes and nod. It makes me like him a little more.

"This mess only gets messier." Magda sighs.

I peek over and spot pupusas in Ramón's bag and my stomach goes wild.

"Yo, Ramón," I whisper. "You mind if I get one of those?"

Ramón looks at his bag then back to me. "Sure."

He takes out a pupusa and tosses it my way. He looks at all the faces staring back at him.

"Fine, come on, everybody get some."

Everybody jumps up to grab pupusas from Ramón's bag and we all sit there silently and eat, mentally preparing for the next part of our mission.

URBAN PROMISE PREP
PRESS RELEASE
FOR IMMEDIATE RELEASE

Wilson Hicks Named Interim Principal

Washington, DC—The community of Urban Promise Prep has come together to honor the memory of its founder and fearless leader, Kenneth Moore, and announce its commitment to continuing forward with building the men of tomorrow as he would've wanted.

Until a permanent replacement is decided upon, Dean Wilson Hicks has been named interim principal, and he takes on this new duty with the solemnity that his predecessor would've expected and desired. Hicks has called for the commission of a portrait of Moore to hang in the entryway of Promise to commemorate the life of this powerful leader.

"We promise. We are the young men of Urban Promise Prep. We are destined for greatness. We are college bound. We are primed for success. We are extraordinary because we work hard. We are respectful, dedicated, committed, and focused. We are our brother's keepers. We are responsible for our futures. We are the future. We promise."

PART FIVE

The Truth

CHAPTER NINETEEN

Break-in

J.B.

Eating something that Ramón made inspires me to try making dinner for my mom. I've only ever warmed things up out of a box or a plastic container of leftovers, but there's something special about homemade food. So I pick the easiest thing I can think of: breakfast. And when she comes home and finds that I made her a scrambled egg sandwich, her smile is so big and surprised that it makes cleaning up slippery egg yolks all worth it.

"You even arranged the fruit all pretty," she says when she sits down to eat.

"I tried," I say.

"What's the occasion?"

"No occasion. I just appreciate you having my back."

I feel bad that I went out to the park today without telling her. But she's got enough on her mind and shoulders—working around the clock in case it turns out we need a lawyer. But that's not why I made her dinner, not because I feel guilty. I just want her to know how grateful I am for her.

"This is really good, J.B.," she says.

"Don't sound so surprised!"

We laugh and eat but don't talk much. It's hard to choose something to talk about when we're surrounded by dread.

After a long silence, my mom finally breaks in. "Can I ask you something?"

"Yes, ma'am."

"What do you remember . . . about that day?" she says eventually, looking down at her plate. "Anything important?"

I know my mom. She doesn't want to look me in my eyes, so I won't see how desperate she is. She's searching for any shred to hang on to, some type of proof that guarantees her baby will stay her baby and not become a man behind bars.

I swallow hard. I can handle all this when I'm just thinking about myself. But when I think about her, that's when it gets tough.

What *do* I remember?

I tell her as much as I can, leaving out stuff I know will hurt her. By the time I get to sitting in detention, I'm aware of how much I've had to not say. I tell her how it was me and two other guys in detention, how I didn't know either of them beyond their faces and names being familiar. But I *don't* tell her that after today at the park, we know each other a lot better. I tell her how Trey left the room to go to the bathroom, and how after Mr. Reggie left to go find Trey, Ramón left to make a phone call. And then, I tell her, *it* happened.

The gunshot. Then everyone flooding into the hallways like ants, including me.

She gasps, as if she wasn't expecting this part of the story. But we both know this was the only possible ending. The facts are the facts.

"So either one of those boys could have done it," she says.

I shrug. *But they say they didn't.*

"Do you remember anything else that day?" she says. "Anything at all?"

"No," I say. What I don't mention is the gun I found. "It was just a normal day. It was the game that night, so people were there taking videos and stuff. There was people like donors and volunteers to put up decorations . . ."

I trail off. I had noticed the people putting up decorations. Paint and streamers and stuff. Some of them I vaguely recognized—parents of some of the guys, teachers, students, including Omar, the kid from the office. Omar. His face sticks like a popcorn kernel now that Trey told me what Solomon saw—Omar coming out of Moore's office.

"What is it?" my mom asks. She must notice something on my face.

"Just thinking about someone."

"Who?"

"Keyana is like a super lawyer detective," I explain—I leave out the part that Keyana is my girl. "She's been helping me try to clear my name."

"And how have y'all been doing that without your phone?" she says, raising her eyebrows higher than the moon.

"Uh . . ."

"You know what, don't tell me," she says, waving her hands. "But I'll say this, you stay out of trouble, you understand me? You need to do everything on the up and up. One wrong move could land you in jail."

I nod silently, thinking, feeling sweat start to crawl down my back. I can't tell my mother that I'm planning to sneak out later and break into the school. Returning to the crime scene to search for what could be the murder weapon.

I know it's a huge risk. But I got to make moves.

The air outside feels cool against my face. I've always loved DC nights, especially when the weather is like this, just right. It's quiet besides the constant wail of sirens, which I hardly hear anymore. I've learned to live with that sound I guess.

A cop car speeds past and instinctually my heart races. It's a shame there's no one here to protect us, only police us. I think about my father. How disappointed he'd be if I ended up in a prison alongside him. Not disappointed with me, but himself.

I shake the thought. No way I'm going to prison for a crime I didn't commit. I kick at a rock on the street to release some tension. Normally I'd throw on a beat, write some bars. Or poetry even. But without my phone, there's nothing to slow my mind down. So, I just let it go, imagining what life could be on the other side of all this mess.

Keyana meets me behind the school wearing a dark hoodie and a black toboggan.

"Why you dressed like a jack boy?" I ask. I can't help but smirk a little.

"This is a boys' school," she says. "I can't walk in there looking like a girl."

I hate to break it to her, but that hoodie and hat don't make her look like a dude. Looking at that fine, hourglass figure, I don't think anything could. But I turn away and keep the thought to myself.

"If we get caught, won't matter if you're a boy, girl, or other. We're screwed. You sure about this? I can always go in myself. In fact, maybe I should. I don't want you any more wrapped up in this than you already are."

Keyana thinks for a moment. It's the first time I see her unsure of anything. She looks in my eyes.

"I'm with you, J.B.," she says.

Without thinking, I give her a hug and she squeezes me tight. It feels so good to have someone I can trust.

"Now how do we get in?" she whispers.

"Follow me. But we have to be extremely careful," I say, handing her a pair of gloves. "Put these on, can't leave any prints."

I take her around back where there's a busted door. But much to my surprise, there's a chain on it with a padlock.

"Shit."

I should've known they'd figure out this door was busted sooner or later.

"Now what?"

I examine the lock. "You wouldn't happen to have any bobby pins would you?"

"How many you need?"

"Two."

Keyana reaches under her hat and digs around in her hair, pulling out exactly what I need.

"Would this work?"

"Perfect."

I flatten one of the pins and go to work jimmying the lock. A skill I picked up busting into lockers at the pool.

After a few thrusts of the bobby pins, the lock pops open. I look at Keyana and she shakes her head.

"I don't even want to know," she says.

I check over my shoulder and open the door as Keyana and I duck into the school, closing the door softly behind us.

Inside, the school is dark and quiet. I take out my flashlight to illuminate the space. I haven't been back in Promise since the shooting, and being here now really spooks me out. Especially since the light only catches the area a few feet in front of us. Every step seems louder than the last, echoing through the empty halls.

"What exactly are we looking for?" Keyana whispers.

"303," I say.

"Huh?"

"Sorry, locker number 303. Luis texted saying that's Omar's locker."

"Oh."

As we head toward the steps leading upstairs, we pass the bathroom where I found the gun. Had someone really used it to commit murder? Or if I go in there right now, will it be where I left it? Untouched and unseen?

I decide to find out. I may never get another chance.

"Remember that gun I told you about?" I whisper.

"Yeah."

"Well, I found it in that bathroom," I say, pointing at the door. I stop and look at Keyana. "I'm sorry. I have to know."

Keyana nods.

I walk over and slowly enter the bathroom, careful not to make any noise.

Inside, the school looks the exact same way it did that day. That damn day, when life at Promise went from bad to worse. The bathroom is quiet, untouched. I go into that same stall, and slowly stand up on the same toilet, peering up at the ceiling. One of the tiles is shifted. I put it back, hadn't I? I know I did.

With trembling hands, I lift it out of the way. I reach my hand inside, patting around. Nothing. Had I pushed it that far? I bring the flashlight up high and stand on my tiptoes on the toilet seat.

It's . . . it's gone. I freeze. My biggest fear is true. I rush out the bathroom to Keyana.

"The gun is gone. Somebody took it! It had to be the gun that was used to kill Moore. And, and I could've stopped it had I just said something."

I stand there stunned. I could have prevented Moore's death. I was so stupid to think I could just hide the gun and everything would be okay. I slide down the wall, burying my face in my hands.

"Fuck. I can't believe this."

Keyana puts her hand on my shoulder. "It's okay. Maybe the murderer didn't find it, the cops did."

"That doesn't help—my prints are still on the gun!"

"Yeah, but if it isn't the murder weapon, I'm sure they'll realize that, right? With ballistics or whatever?"

She makes a good point. But still, I have my doubts. Murder weapon or not, my prints on a gun wouldn't look good.

"Bottom line, we can't stop here. We have to keep looking."

She makes another good point and I cut the pity party.

"You're right. Let's go."

When we arrive at Omar's locker, I know just what to do. I've broken into my own locker a million times and Omar's is just as easy. I slip the ballpoint pen from my back pocket, jam it into the side of the built-in lock, and twist it counterclockwise three times. When it pops open, Keyana gives me a look.

"Not what you think," I say.

She raises her eyebrows and pokes her lips out and I try not to laugh again. Instead I turn to Omar's locker and shine my flashlight in.

"What a mess," she whispers.

It is. Papers spilling everywhere, photos and articles in stacks that could fall out any second.

"We gotta be quick," I say, glancing up and down the hallway, like someone might spring out and catch us at any moment.

I pull out a stack of binders while trying to keep the rest from toppling. Keyana steps up to catch the falling pile of school supplies while I sift through the papers.

A stack slips out of one of the binders and onto the floor with a thud. We both freeze and I cut off my flashlight.

"You hear anything?" I whisper.

"Just you," Keyana snaps back.

After we confirm we're alone, I turn my flashlight back on.

"What was that?" she says.

I bend down to pick up whatever fell and freeze in horror.

It's dozens of weird photos of Principal Moore in the halls, outside the school, and even at his house.

"Okayyyy," says Keyana, "that isn't creepy at all."

"Why in the world would he have these pictures of Moore in his locker?"

Keyana and I look at each other, both thinking the same thing.

"What else is in there? Maybe some evidence that strongly ties him to the murder? Maybe even a gun?"

I look up at Keyana when she says the word *gun*.

"What, just saying. If we're lucky."

I shake my head and keep looking through the stacks of paper until something catches my eye.

"What? What is it?"

"Look," I say, turning the document around.

"It's from Moore," she says with surprise. "*Your request for Promise Fund monies has been denied. Using the funds for photography materials would be an inappropriate use of funds with college application projects as the aim. Promise Fund monies are not to be used for personal projects.*"

"So Omar requested money from the Promise Fund and Moore said no," I whisper.

Keyana looks at me with a serious expression.

"I wonder what Omar was doing in Moore's office that day. Do you think—"

Just then we hear a door close. We glance up and see a beam of light coming from around the corner.

"Oh shit, they must have security here. Quick, hide!"

I pull Keyana into a nearby crevice in front of the music room. I try the door, but it's locked. We squeeze even closer. So close I can feel her against me. Hard as it is pressed up against her, I try to concentrate on not making a sound.

The beam of light moves closer toward us, and now I can hear the hard-bottom shoes of the security guard approaching. I look Keyana in her eyes and I can tell she's scared. She has way more to lose than I do.

"I got an idea, just trust me."

I dig in my pocket and pull out a coin.

"Wait—"

Before she can finish, I toss the coin as far as I can down the hall and pull her down to the floor with me.

As soon as the coin lands with a *ping*, I see the guard's flashlight swivel in that direction. I hope they'll take the bait and start walking that way. But then the guard stops moving. Staying put like they're searching for something. Or *someone*.

For a second, all I can think about is getting caught. Making myself look guilty while all I was doing was trying to prove my innocence.

Just when I'm thinking about grabbing Keyana and running, the guard starts moving again. His footsteps quicken as he rushes past us.

"They're gone," I whisper as low as I can. "Grab the binders and let's get the hell out of here."

We grab what we can from Omar's locker before we hightail it. It's starting to feel like we may have a number one suspect.

CHAPTER TWENTY

The Talk

TREY

N ICO MARTINEZ
I type the name online to see what I can find.

After seeing Mrs. Hall with Detective Bo, I thought it may be a little too risky to keep tailing her. I need to think of another way to get more info on her. But in the meantime, one of the other names struck me. Nico.

I knew of all the other suspects but Nico, so I figured I'd get familiar. A few profiles pop up on my computer screen, but none of them are the Nico I'm looking for. I click around a few more pages, but it seems pointless. I switch over to the "images" online and scroll through until I see a familiar face. I click on the image to enlarge it. It's Nico.

Except it's not the same Nico I'm used to. This Nico has hard eyes and shaved hair, exposing the skull tattoo on the back of his head. The image is from a court case.

"Nico Martinez charged with an attempted murder in connection with Martinez's gang affiliation, Dioses del Humo," I whisper.

I can't believe it! Nico is a member of Dioses del Humo?!

A flash of rage washes over me. Ramón had to know Nico. Now Ramón's uneasiness makes sense. He looked down at his feet when we said Nico's name, like he was hiding something. Why would he hold back unless he was involved somehow?

I hear Uncle T's footsteps coming down the hall and slam my laptop shut. I pretend to be asleep. I'd rather not be bothered if I don't have to be.

"Trey, you decent?"

I'm shocked. Uncle T has never asked me something like that. Usually, he just barges in whenever he feels like it. I'm so shocked I forget I'm supposed to be pretending to sleep.

"Yeah," I call out as I sit up in bed.

Uncle T walks in and sits at the foot of my bed. He seems more tired than usual.

"Trey. I just got a call and I think it's time we spoke."

My heart sinks.

"A call about what?" I ask.

"The police said they identified the type of gun that was used on your principal. They looked into weapons registered to this address and found mine, which apparently matches the make and model of the gun used on Moore."

I can't even look at my uncle. I just start crying without warning.

Honestly, it feels good. A release. The secret had been weighing so heavy on me and I didn't even realize it. My biggest fear is true. I am in some way responsible for the death of Principal Moore.

I take some comfort in thinking that whoever killed Moore may have still done it, with or without my uncle's gun. But I definitely nudged them along.

As he stares at me crying, Uncle T's calmness terrifies me. I feel like at any moment he could just turn and strangle me to literal death.

Put me out of my misery.

"I told the police I checked for my gun and did not find it," Uncle T continues. "I also told them it could've been stolen and I hadn't noticed since I haven't used it recently. Of course, that won't really hold. It's all too clean."

I can't meet his eyes.

"You're here, your principal is shot, and my gun is missing. Look at me, Trey."

I hear something I've never heard in his voice. An air of concern. Or even fear maybe. I look at him.

"Where is the gun, Trey?"

"I don't know. I grabbed your bag by accident that morning."

"Why didn't you come back home?"

"I didn't want to be late to school—I would've been benched for the game."

"Why didn't you call?"

"I didn't want you mad at me. So I hid the gun in case they did a locker check. But when I went back to find it, it was gone."

My uncle looks away from me. For a long time, too, like he was either thinking of what to say, or hiding his face in shame. I couldn't tell.

"I'm sorry, Trey," he said. Finally looking back my way. "I . . . I think I failed you if you think you can't talk to me when you're in trouble. I only wanted you to be great, son. Great. You don't have time, Trey. You don't have time to be a knucklehead. And I've been trying to force you to be a man the only way I know how. The way my father showed me. But maybe I was wrong. And now maybe it will cost you your life. I'm sorry. I'll figure something out."

My uncle stands up and leaves, closing the door softly behind him. I wipe my face.

I think about Coach shouting, *Get your head in the game, Jackson!* Will I ever play again? I think about what Solomon's punk ass said online: that joke about me playing ball in jail. Is that really my future? To just get thrown away like so many people do? My whole life? My whole future?

So, they matched the bullet to the same kind of gun that I accidentally took to school that day. But they haven't actually found the gun. Yet. And I think I might know where it is.

CHAPTER TWENTY-ONE

Nico

RAMÓN

Death can feel far away until it happens right in front of you.

People assume that because you grew up in gang territory, you're numb to stuff like what happened to Mr. Moore. That's just not true. Ever since it happened, I feel like my body is filled with floodwater. I learned when I was little to never walk through those still oceans: They're filled with filth, and sometimes electricity, so if you're not careful you could get shocked.

I'm not supposed to leave the house, but inside I can't sit still. I know I need to look more into Nico, but I've been stalling because I'm scared of what I might find. And terrified of what the Dioses will do to me if they catch me in the act. So I hang out on the back porch, alternating between sitting and pacing.

I've just sat down when my phone vibrates loudly against the hard porch. I snatch it up.

It's a group text from Keyana.

> We need to find the murder weapon. The only way to prove who did it is to find the gun, right? It would have the killer's fingerprints. It would explain everything.

I try to swallow my anger. I type back quickly:

> You make it sound so easy. It's not that simple.

No one answers, no matter how long I keep staring at the screen. I drop it back on the porch in frustration. I think back to Ever and that exchange with Nico at 314 Bosetti. Maybe it is that easy. Time to stop stalling.

I stand up like lightning, all the electrified floodwater shocking my spine.

"¿Podría ser?" I breathe. I look at the clock. Plenty of time before Abuela gets home. What was the name of that restaurant I saw Nico at again? I google the address, 314 Bosetti, and there it is, El Rincón.

I dial the number to the spot and after a few rings a soft voice picks up on the other line.

"Hello and thank you for calling El Rincón. This is Anabel speaking, how may I help you?"

I deepen my voice to try to sound older. "Yes, is Nico there tonight? I need to drop something off for him."

"Yes, I believe he's still here. I know his shift ends soon. Did you want to speak to him?"

Immediately I hang up the phone. This could be the guy.

My shoes are already on and my phone is already in my hand. I grab my pocketknife, just in case, and run out the front door, hoping that somehow Nico will lead me to the murder weapon.

The night is unusually silent. I figure I'll follow Nico home, see where he lives. Then, at some point, go do a little digging and see what I find in the house. If I come up with the weapon, that's it, I'm free. If not, maybe there's something else in there that gives some sort of clue as to what happened to Mr. Moore.

The restaurant is close enough to walk to and I could use the fresh air. As I approach the building, I see him. Nico Martinez, leaving the restaurant in his kitchen uniform, apron tossed over his shoulder after a long day of work.

For a brief moment I actually start to feel bad for the guy. Does he work at Promise and then come work at another place? Reminds me of my abuela, always working. The hustle is real.

Nico walks down the street and I do the same, careful to maintain a safe distance even though it's dark out and he won't notice me.

He passes a bus stop which makes me thinks he lives in the area. Even better. Then he hits a hard right down an alley.

Not the safest of places to follow someone you think is a murderer, but what choice do I have? If we don't solve this case soon, they're likely to put it on all of us.

I turn into the alley and stop in my tracks. Nico is gone.

I squint my eyes, staring through the light fog, but there's no sign of Nico.

"Impossible," I whisper to myself.

I slowly creep down the alley, looking at the building surrounding me. All dark and empty with no sign of life, let alone Nico.

I get halfway down the alley when it hits me. Nico lost me on purpose. But why? What is he hiding?

Dread slides down my spine—what if he saw my face?

I start to turn around to hurry back the way I came when suddenly I'm shoved hard from behind and pushed to the ground. I land with a thud, pulling out my switchblade to ward off the mugger.

But before I can get up, the cold barrel of a pistol presses against the back of my head.

"Fuck are you doing following me!"

It's no mugger at all. It's a murderer. It's Nico.

"No, please, I'm sorry!"

I'm shocked that he picked up on me so fast. Then again, the streets teach you to be aware of your surroundings. I should've known I was no match.

"Talk!" he yells, pressing the gun harder against my skull.

"I . . . I . . ."

I don't know what to say. The truth? Do you tell a potential murderer you're onto them? In a dark alley where nobody can hear you? I was all out of options.

"Nico," I call out. "That's your name, right?! Mr. Martinez?"

It's silent for a moment. Suddenly I feel the gun pull away and see a hand reach out. I grab it, and Nico helps me to my feet.

I expect to see him pointing the barrel of his gun right at me. But wait . . . he doesn't have a gun at all. It was just his knuckle digging into my head.

Nico squints as he tries to see me in the dark.

"Ramón. Ramón, what the hell are you doing? Why are you out here this time of night? Why are you tailing me?!"

I slowly back away to put some distance between us. "I'm . . . I'm sorry. I just wanted to talk."

"About what?" Nico looks around as if I'm setting him up. I can tell he's pissed.

I never considered it but, if Nico isn't the killer, he probably suspects me just as much as I suspect him.

"I didn't know you were Dioses."

"That was a while ago."

"You've done time?"

"Yeah, so?"

I can't outright ask him if he's a murderer, so I fumble for a way to find out more. "It's just I saw you with Ever earlier."

"What?"

"Ever. He gave you a package. Looked like money."

"How long you've been following me, kid?"

"Just then . . . and now."

"For what?"

"Well . . . I mean, you're affiliated. Moore got my cousin César arrested and Dioses wanted revenge. So I thought . . ."

Nico sighs and shakes his head as if he's disappointed he's been found out.

"You don't know shit, little man," he says, taking a step toward me.

I stand my ground and stare him in the eyes, waiting for him to say more.

"Since I got a record and used to be a Dios, you think I killed Moore?"

So much for trying to skirt around the truth. I nod, one hand locked on my switchblade in case something's about to go down.

Nico rubs his chin and lets out a chuckle before he continues. "Funny enough, the money you saw me get from Ever was a down payment on El Rincón. I guess César heard the place was selling and wanted to move quick to keep it in the neighborhood. Had nothing to do with Moore."

I can't believe my ears. Now it makes sense what César said right before he got arrested. *"Maybe there's another option. Another storefront, you know?"* He had the whole thing already worked out.

I feel proud and sad all at once.

Proud of my primo for seriously considering changing his life-style. Proud of myself for getting through to him. But I'm sad I even had to suspect the Dioses for this in the first place. A lot of them are trying to find their path. They weren't able to go to an Urban Promise Prep.

"I'm sorry, sir. I . . . I don't know what to say. I'm freaking out, you know?"

I have the sudden stupid urge to cry. I rub my face extra hard to push it away. For some reason, Nico rubs his eyes too.

"You got a lawyer?" he asks.

"Yeah, but he's hard to get ahold of."

Nico just shakes his head again.

"Don't let them get you with this," he says, turning away. "Do everything you can. And when shit like this goes down, always best to start by following the money."

"What do you mean?"

"Look, I don't know much," Nico replies. "But we cafeteria staff talk, and there's no way the school needs to be pinching pennies with so much sponsorship and grant money coming in."

"You think someone's stealing money from the school?"

"Like I said, I don't know much. But if it was me, I'd find a way to dig deeper."

With that, Nico turns around and starts walking away.

"Thanks," I choke out, but he's already near the mouth of the alley. He's almost out of sight when I call after him: "I'm sorry."

He pauses, and I almost think he's going to ignore me. But he looks at me over his shoulder. "Me too."

And then he's gone.

BREAKING NEWS:

THE PROMISE MURDER INVESTIGATION

In their ongoing investigation, police have used ballistic evidence to identify the type of weapon used in the shooting. They have been able to conclude the type of pistol used matches the caliber of weapon owned by one of the guardians of the three suspects.

We've reached out for comments about this discovery but the person, who has asked to remain anonymous, declined to answer.

Stay tuned for more updates on the Promise murder.

CHAPTER TWENTY-TWO

Confusion

TREY

The day after we met up at the park, I get a message from Ramón that he wants us to meet again, later tonight. My whole chest lights up. Of course I want to meet. Because now I know he was holding things back about what happened that day, and I'm sure as hell going to find out the truth.

The trick is waiting for my uncle to go to sleep. And my mom too, because her coming along on this little trip ain't happening this time. My uncle has never stayed up late—early to bed, early to rise. Military man always. But waiting for him to bunk down is like waiting for water to boil.

Meanwhile, it's me that's bubbling over. I was just beginning to trust Ramón. The worst feeling in the world is having your trust betrayed. Especially when you're like me and don't trust many people to begin with. When Keyana texts saying she and J.B. are on the way to the meet-up, I'm literally pacing back and forth in my room. I can't wait to confront Ramón about Nico.

I watch the clock. 9:38. My mom's lights are off. My uncle is usually out like clockwork at nine thirty, so I make my move.

I finally hop out my window, the chill of the night creeping across my neck. I put up my hood and head toward the bodega where Ramón wants to meet. I jog, but not too fast. I don't want to be exhausted when I run up on Ramón.

I'm expecting to find everybody chilling and waiting on me when I roll up, but before I even turn onto the block, I can hear them shouting. It's too dark to really see what's going on, so I put on my boosters and sprint down the street, ready to jump in—at this point I don't really care against who.

"What's going on?" I ask, rolling up on the group.

They all freeze and turn to me.

"We should ask you!" Ramón says when he realizes it's me. Then Keyana and J.B. turn to me too.

"What the hell are you talking about?" I yell back, caught off guard.

"Don't play dumb!" Ramón shouts. "Somebody is lying and it ain't me."

"Me either. I'll introduce you to my mom if you'd like, she ain't never even owned a gun," J.B. says.

"My abuela either," Ramón adds.

"Trey?" Magda says softly. "Did you see the news?"

I can feel my heart stop.

J.B. turns on me with his eyes narrowed—Keyana too.

"I haven't seen it—what happened?" I say quickly.

Just as fast as I say it, Keyana is pulling up an article. I pretend to read it, but I know what it says. My uncle and I just spoke about it, but I didn't imagine the news would be made public. Not this quick at least.

"I . . . I don't know—"

"You liar! You did this, didn't you?!" Ramón jumps at me. J.B. steps between us to hold him back.

I'm at a loss for words. The pressure gets to me and I don't think I can hold it in any longer.

"It . . . it was an accident . . . ," I cough out.

"You *did* do it!" Ramón yells, almost like he can't believe it. "You killed him! You killed Principal Moore!"

"NO I didn't!" I roar. "That's not the accident I mean! *Bringing the gun* was the accident! I didn't kill nobody! I tried to hide it . . ."

"Hide *what*?!"

"The gun!" I explain how I accidentally took my uncle's bag. "So rather than go home and get suspended from the game, I went into school through the basement door to miss the metal detectors out front, and stashed the gun in the basement bathroom. But when I went back to find it, it was gone. Somebody took it."

"That's a bullshit story," Ramón says, bristling, looking at all the other faces around us, urging them to attack me too. "He's lying—"

"He's not lying," J.B. interrupts, then looks down at the ground.

I turn on him with surprise.

"He couldn't have shot Moore with that gun." J.B. looks directly at me. "You hid it in the toilet tank, right?"

I stare at him in disbelief, then nod slowly.

"Yeah," he whispers, and Keyana stares at him too, wordless. "I found it. And I thought somebody was gonna shoot the school up. So, I hid it in the ceiling, thinking nobody would find it. There's no way Trey would've known where the gun was."

I could almost hug J.B. in that moment.

"See! When I asked to go to the bathroom during detention, I went to find it so I could bring it back home. And the next thing I knew, somebody was shooting."

"So *that's* where you went during detention?" Ramón says. But then he turns on J.B. before I can even reply. "So, you had the gun—"

But now I cut *him* off.

"I know *you're* not accusing nobody," I snap. "Tell us who Nico Martinez really is, Ramón."

"Huh?" Ramón says.

"You heard me. Tell us who Nico is."

Magda turns to Ramón. "What is he talking about?"

"Yeah, what's up with Nico?" J.B. asks.

Ramón sighs. All that energy subsiding. "Nico was a Dios."

The news drops like a bomb on the group.

"Hold up," J.B. shouts. "The guy with the criminal record, the guy *you* wanted to check out, is in your gang?"

"And he has an attempted murder charge," I belt out.

"I didn't know that part," Ramón says. "And, it's not *my* gang. The guy is clean, I checked him out. He's on the straightened path."

"Now who's bullshitting?" I snarl.

"Ramón, did you know this before? When you said you'd look into Nico?" Keyana asks.

"I did. But the only reason I didn't say anything was because I knew it'd make me look suspicious. But it couldn't have been Nico; in fact, he wasn't even there at the time of the shooting. He was already at his other gig. I checked."

"You should've said something," Magda whispers.

"I needed all the info first so I could explain! It's no different from Trey not telling us about the gun. Or J.B. not telling us about the gun for that matter—and we still don't know what he did with it. Or why he had blood on his shirt!"

Suddenly, a voice from the dark stops us all cold. It takes me a minute to recognize it, but then Unk steps out of the shadows.

"You youngbloods need to use your heads," he says. "I thought that school was supposed to make you smart."

I'm about to yell at him to mind his business, but J.B. speaks first.

"What you mean, Unk?"

"What I *mean* is that if you were as smart as y'all are supposed to be, you would see that somebody is trying to make it look like one of y'all did this. Better pay attention," Unk says, sipping on something inside a brown paper bag. Then he disappears back into the shadows as if he was never there.

"He's right, y'all. If we don't trust each other, we're never going to get through this. Somebody else is pulling the strings. We have to tell each other everything. It's the only way," Keyana says.

She makes a good point. We all sit there in silence.

J.B. kicks at the ground as if there's more he wants to say. "I get anxiety nosebleeds," J.B. whispers. It's the first time I've seen him unsure of himself. "When I get nervous, I sweat and sometimes my nose bleeds. That's why I had blood on me that day. The gunshot just triggered it."

"It really doesn't help that all our stories sound like bullshit," I say.

Everybody chuckles. It feels good being able to find my funny again.

"And I don't know what happened to the gun. Same thing as Trey, I went back for it and it was gone. I just checked when we looked into Omar," J.B. says.

"Omar?" Magda asks.

"Yep, Omar," J.B. jumps in. "Me and Keyana went to Promise and searched Omar's locker. We found some disturbing stuff. It's what we wanted to show you tonight before . . ." J.B. turns to me. "You know."

J.B. pulls out a binder and opens it. It's full of all sorts of notes on Principal Moore. Places he worked, where he lived. There were even photos of Moore. Around the school and even going in and out of his house.

"What the hell are these?" Ramón asks before I can.

"These were in Omar's locker. Along with this."

J.B. hands a document to Magda.

"Says he was denied funding from the Promise Fund."

J.B. nods. "But the weird thing is, even though it's a stash of money to pay for college for any Promise student that can't afford it, I've never heard of any student getting a grant. Besides, Moore always kicks out any student who isn't on track to get a scholarship based on academics or financial needs."

"If that's true, it sounds like some sort of scam. Where does that money go if not to the students?" Keyana asks.

It was a great question. One we hadn't thought to ask.

"Nico told me to follow the money," Ramón says. "That things just don't add up since Promise is taking in so much donor money, but no one knows where it's being used." He pauses, like he's trying to work something out in his head. "Can you imagine if Ennis found out the money he was bringing into Promise was just a scam?"

"Can you imagine if he was in on it?"

We all shudder at the thought of the conspiracy.

"Keyana asked a great question. Where does the money go? If we can figure that out, it may be a clue," J.B. says. "There has to be a log of something like that."

"What about this Omar kid?" Magda adds. "He's sounding more and more shady. Not only does he have all these stalkerish photos of Moore, but it sounds like he also had beef with him about the denied grant money."

"I had the same thought," J.B. says. "And I know a way to kill two birds with one stone."

I look at J.B. and I can tell he's thinking the same thing I am. We have to talk to Omar.

Magdalena Peña

t's almost as if whoever really did this, did it knowing that there would be plenty of suspects to throw the cops off their trail. Are murderers who get away with it always smart? Or do they get lucky?

After we left the bodega, I got home to find César on the couch watching TV. The house arrest monitor is still locked around his ankle. On TV, the local anchor is talking about the upcoming memorial that Promise Prep is putting on for Moore. It's all eerie. I stare for a while, silent.

"Aren't you glad you never went to Promise?" I say eventually, hoping he laughs. I'm relieved when he does. It seems like I haven't heard him laugh in a long, long time.

"Definitely," he says. "Bunch of gangsters in there."

We laugh some more, but I can't help but feel sad. Everything is such a mess, and even though I believe more than ever that my cousin is innocent—and, now that I know them, J.B. and Trey too—things have only gotten more complicated.

And unless we can make a breakthrough soon, one of them is going to jail.

On the TV, the shiny-toothed anchor drones on and on: "The

celebration of this incredible man's life will include the unveiling of the portrait commissioned by his successor, Wilson Hicks, interim president. He will preside over the ceremony, where community leaders will ask us all to come together to honor the accomplishments and legacy of DC's one and only Kenneth Moore."

"Who do you think did it?" I ask César when it cuts to commercial.

He's silent for so long I think he either didn't hear me or is choosing to ignore me. But when he speaks, he's shrugging, staring down at his ankle monitor.

"This kind of murder is about power," he says. "When powerful men are killed, it's always about power. A lot of dudes from the streets go to Promise. Somebody wanted Moore to know he wasn't really the king."

"Seems like being on the throne is dangerous," I say.

"Exhausting," he answers.

He sounds so tired. I scoot over a little bit and rest my head on his shoulder, like I used to. My brother doesn't move away.

Nobody

can't say anything.
   I have too much to lose.
   Sometimes the key to survival is staying invisible.

Keyana Glenn

t's midnight when Magda texts the whole group:

> Who wanted to prove that Moore wasn't king?

I send off my reply:

> Everybody keep your eyes open for answers to that question today.

I've been doing a lot of research, and if I've learned one thing, it's this: Money makes the world go round. And not just the world, but schools. And especially schools like Promise.

I mean, it's already bullshit that some schools get more help than others in the first place. And somehow, schools with kids who look like me always seem to get the short end of the stick. It's just like everything else in this world, and it makes me not only want to be a lawyer, but a lawmaker or something.

But prep schools like Promise are another thing, and as I sit on my bed swiping through my phone, I learn more and more. Principals like Moore can quickly become rock stars, and it's almost like one of those evangelical preachers that gets famous speaking the word and then goes on tour saving souls under a spotlight.

I find dozens of articles chronicling his rise in DC. He was so beloved. I find pictures of him, old and new, with teachers, parents, and students. In one he stands beaming with Mrs. Hall. Her smile is so big it looks like it might crack. The photo was taken when Promise first opened. The quote under the picture was about how proud Mrs. Hall was to be joining Moore on "this endeavor."

"Yeah," I mutter under my breath, thinking of what Moore did to J.B. "This endeavor of trying to fight teenagers like they're grown men."

The more I learn about Moore and his career path, the more I start to get a fuller picture of who he was. Beyond the bullshit rules that he enforced harder and harder at Promise, he seemed like the kind of guy who liked to be admired. In some ways he wasn't that different from the Mercy girls coming to tutor the boys in ESL. He looked at dudes like J.B. and Trey and Ramón and saw something . . . *wrong* with them. Something that needed to be crushed into a box, breaking all the bones to make them fit.

Maybe they reminded him of something he didn't like about himself.

It makes it hard to look at all the smiling photos of Moore in suits—at benefits, at fundraisers, at Capitol Hill events shaking hands and getting patted on the back and grinning at the camera—when guys like J.B. aren't even allowed to smile if they're inside Promise's walls. That he gets a nosebleed and it's written into his permanent record that he got into a fight.

I put my phone to sleep, letting my mind wander. Inside Promise's walls, Moore was king, and no one challenged him. Inside a kingdom, the king can say or do no wrong. When you hear about a king being toppled, like in *Game of Thrones*, the threat often comes from inside the kingdom.

My thoughts go immediately to Stanley Ennis.

According to what I can find, Ennis is a king in his own right. He funds expeditions into jungles and up mountains, owns lots of businesses, and donates enough to get things named after him.

But when the threatening emails were released, I thought it didn't sound like him. *"You were supposed to be there for me, and you decided to turn your back."*

I look outside at the quiet street, and I can't help but imagine the neighborhood as a potential territory, not of a gang like Dioses del Humo, but of politicians and school boards and aldermen and principals and all the people that posed in photos with Principal Moore, hyping him up as the savior of "lost boys," meanwhile he was drilling the joy out of them. This is all their kingdom, people like Stanley Ennis—pay to build a gym at a school, then bring in boys to play in it. Toy soldiers, chess pieces, moved around a board while they rake in state funding. I had no idea there was so much money in schools like Promise until I started reading about Moore and his kingly career.

I pull out my phone once again and text the group.

> Promise Boys, when is the next game day for the basketball team? We need to find a way to tail Ennis and learn more.

CHAPTER TWENTY-THREE

Confrontation

J.B.

M e, Trey, and Ramón wait up the block from Promise just before dismissal. Trey even brought his binoculars so we can keep our distance but also see the front door. I have to say, working with Trey and Ramón was starting to have its perks.

We figure we'll wait for Omar to leave school, and then confront him to see what's what. I don't think this kid will be a problem, but I can't shake the fact that if he's the shooter, he may still have that gun on him. He'd need to use it on me if we get to boxing.

I didn't know Omar well, but I know the kid is creepy. He never spoke, never really even looked your way. Finding all those photos of Moore freaked me out. I hate to say it but I could totally see him pulling the trigger.

We all wore our uniforms to blend in as kids pour into the street. Trey's idea, but I doubt it works. I look at my watch. 5:00 P.M. Any moment now. And right on cue, the school bell sounds off and Promise boys flood the streets. Itching to get out of that place.

"There he is," Ramón calls out.

He nods to a skinny kid walking down the steps.

"Yep, that's him. Looks like he's coming this way," I say.

We duck behind the wall of the school as Omar walks toward us. When he passes, we start on his trail.

"When should we move on him?" Ramón asks.

"Soon as the coast is clear," I say. "He's probably walking to the bus, just gotta get to him before there."

We walk a few more blocks before we're clear of the Promise crowd. It's just us and Omar on the street.

"Now's our chance." I lengthen my strides to catch Omar.

I hear Ramón and Trey quicken their pace too. As I get closer, I realize Omar has his earphones in and can't hear me. I use that to my advantage and get right up on him. I reach out for his book bag and snatch it off his back, making sure I get that gun away from him in case he has it. He whips around.

"Yo, what you doing!" he squeaks out. But when he sees the three of us standing there, he breaks out into a run.

"Shit, get him!" I shout.

We sprint after Omar for a few more blocks. I have to admit, the kid's fast. Probably from running from bullies his whole life. Trey finally catches up and tackles him to the ground. Ramón and I run up shortly after, standing over Omar, trying to catch our breath.

"What the hell are y'all doing?" he cries out.

"We could ask you the same. Why you running?"

"You mean from the three suspected murderers that seem to want to attack me? Oh, I don't know. What do you want?"

His fire surprises me. I expected him to cower but he doesn't.

"Explain this," I say, taking out his binder.

"My binder! How did you get this?"

"Never mind how I got it. Why do you have these images of Moore? And tell us what you know about the Promise Fund."

Omar's face changes, as if he knows something we don't. He stands up and brushes himself off. He looks around and I can't tell if he's checking for help or to make sure we're alone. He takes a step toward us and leans in.

"None of you did this, did you?"

We all look at each other.

"No, we didn't," I reply. "But we can't say the same for you. We hear you were the last person seen with Moore. And according to that letter, you had motive."

Omar shakes his head.

"You don't know what you're in the middle of. I have those images of Moore because I was doing a piece on him for the school board. He was lobbying for another Promise campus and wanted to make a presentation."

Omar scratches his brow nervously as he takes a deep breath, preparing to continue.

"I figured I should at least get some new camera equipment, but he told me this was an opportunity for me. That when the board saw my work, they'd maybe support me in college or some shit. But I started to see things. Like, despite being told the Promise Fund is exclusively for tuition help, the board requires funds be accessible to all students for a number of reasons: books, uniforms, extracurricular equipment, not just college. Moore never told us that. So when he denied my request I knew something was up."

Omar paused, checking over his shoulder. We did the same. We seemed to be alone, so he continued.

"I started following him outside of our sessions. Moore was unraveling. He was stealing money from the fund."

It was like a bomb drop. Principal Moore always preached perfection, excellence, and discipline, but it was all a lie. Honestly, I'm disappointed. Whatever Moore was doing may have gotten him killed.

"I believe somebody found out about what he was doing and started threatening him."

"Those emails," Ramón says.

"Exactly. Whoever did this knew what he was doing and didn't like it."

Me and the fellas exchange a glance. Omar's story sounds pretty legit, especially considering the information we already had. Don't mean it's the truth, though.

"Well, hold on, what about you being seen with Moore before the murder?" I ask.

"I told you, he had me doing this piece on him. I was going to interview him that evening. It was the last part of the project. I was in his office trying to set up the mic but needed some tape to get it to stick. I left his office and before I could even find my tape, I heard the shot. Look," Omar says as he pulls a flyer from his pocket.

It's a vigil for Moore.

"I'm going to be playing the tape we worked on at this, you have to believe me."

We all stand there staring at the flyer to commemorate Moore's untimely death. Remembering what it was like to hear a gunshot in the last place you'd expect. Violence in my city was so common, but I never expected it behind the walls of Promise. Not like this. It just reminded me that we're not safe anywhere.

"You all have any other suspects?" Omar asks.

"We thought Dioses could've been responsible," I say, looking at Ramón. "Word was Moore got a general arrested and they have a couple inside guys. But that was a dead end."

"There's still Mrs. Hall too. She showed up to Promise the day Moore was killed and she's married to one of the cops on the case. Pretty suspicious," Trey adds.

Omar looks up.

"I don't think Mrs. Hall could've done it. I saw her headed to the game just before the shot went off."

Trey, Ramón, and I exchange a glance. As much as it stung to lose one more suspect, checking Mrs. Hall off the list felt like a step in the right direction. I break the silence.

"Well, if not Mrs. Hall, and not you, and not the Dioses, I guess that leaves . . . Ennis. Stanley Ennis. He's a big donor to the Promise Fund and he's the last person on the visitation log for Moore."

Omar's face lights up.

"I know him! He's always asking me to shoot sizzle reel for the basketball games. And as I've been looking more into the Promise Fund, I discovered something today. Can I, uh . . . can I see my book bag?"

I stare at Omar, wondering if I can trust him. I take a look inside the book bag to make sure there's no weapon in there. It's only school supplies and a couple camera lenses.

"Sorry, bro. Here you go," I say, handing over Omar's bag.

He digs through the bag, combing through loose papers until he finds what he's looking for.

"Okay. Here it is. I was able to tap into the system and see what requests had been accepted and denied from the Promise Fund. There's a lot of nos. Pretty much all nos. But there's one kid who *always* gets the money he asks for. Look at the name."

Omar turns the page around and points. Stan Lee.

"Stan Lee. Like the Marvel guy?" I ask.

"Yeah, or like . . . the donor guy. Stanley Ennis. Guys, there is no Stan Lee at our school. Stanley Ennis is the biggest donor, right? Funds are being stolen and somehow a kid that doesn't go here is always getting withdrawals from *our* money? Either Stanley was stealing from the school and Moore had to pay up, maybe Ennis was even blackmailing him, or Moore was stealing for himself and using a name like Stanley's to throw anyone off his trail. Either way, only one of those guys is still breathing."

The pieces all fall into place. Stanley and Moore were running some sort of operation, the business went south, and somebody had to pay the price. No different from in the streets.

"There's a game today," Trey says without even thinking. "Ennis is probably in the school right now."

Brandon Jenkins

When Trey texted me asking to do him a favor, I almost said no. My mom still doesn't know we've been talking. If she found out, she'd go ballistic. But he's my boy. I play the one, he plays the two. And I already did him wrong by icing him out. I kind of owe him one.

But damn, I should have said no.

I should be heading to practice. But instead I had to be a fool and agree to follow Stanley Ennis after school. When I asked Trey what the hell for, he just said this was all to find the truth about who killed Mr. Moore. And again, I owe him.

So that's how I've spent the last forty-five minutes: hiding in the locker room, the bathroom, anywhere to avoid Mr. Reggie while he sweeps the school to make sure everyone but the athletes are gone, and waiting for Mr. Ennis to leave. I don't know how the hell Trey expects me to follow him once we get outside—it's not like I'm James Bond, or like I have a stack of disguises. Plus, Ennis knows me way too well—if he sees me and recognizes me he's just going to ask me straight up what the hell I'm doing. And everybody knows I'm a terrible liar.

So, there I am, hiding in the conference room, trying to keep my feet from falling asleep, and texting Trey to tell him this is a terrible idea, when I hear voices coming closer. This conference room is right by the door Mr. Ennis always leaves through—he parks his Porsche in the side lot where the cameras are—so I know one of the voices has to be his.

The conference room has glass windows on all four sides, so if they're coming from the wrong angle, they will absolutely look in and see me.

"It's a lot to take on!" Ennis is saying. Thank God—they're coming from the hallway behind me and they won't see me unless they come inside. "But you're a man of strategy."

I assume Mr. Ennis is talking to Coach, as that's usually who he talks to when he comes to practice. Mr. Ennis likes to see how his *investment* is going. The more games we win, the happier he is. I'm never really sure why guys like Mr. Ennis care so much about high school sports, but with him specifically I always assumed he's trying to relive his youth or something.

"You just need to hold down the fort," Ennis is saying. "You've got a big job ahead of you, but if anyone can handle it, it's you."

My heart starts to pound. I know in movies people always get caught because of something stupid like their phone ringing. My phone is *always* on silent, but I check just in case, then stuff it in my hoodie pocket, trying not to breathe too loudly.

"I appreciate your confidence," the person Ennis is talking to says. The voice is familiar, but he's talking low, so I can't quite place it. "It's going to be a hard transition for all of us, but we'll muddle through."

"We'll do more than muddle," Ennis says, chuckling. I hear a rustle of paper. "This is all you need right here. Just make sure nothing gets interrupted and it will all smooth out."

"Smooth is good." I recognize the voice now—Dean Hicks. *Principal*

Hicks. I'm close enough to the door where I could lean over and peek, but I don't dare. "I just plan to stay the course. Who knows, maybe even make some improvements."

"Well, you know that's what I like to hear!" I can tell Ennis is smiling from ear to ear just from his voice. Then he lowers his voice to almost a whisper. "I hope you're willing to do what it takes to make this partnership worth it. For both of us."

"I've always been a businessman," Hicks answers. "That's why Moore hired me. Cut through the bullshit."

"Well, that's exactly what we need—especially with the Promise Fund. Smoothing that out too?"

"Doing my best."

"Good. We can pick up where Moore left off. How are you holding up? Any arrests yet?"

"Not that I know of. But we know one of those boys did it. It's only a matter of time. Maybe soon they can apply some pressure, get them to turn on each other, you know?"

That makes my stomach turn, but Ennis makes a sound of agreement. "Well, they need to find the gun! All these police they've had in and out of the school—not great press, I've gotta say. They need to search high and low, find it, then make a damn arrest! Then we can be done with this whole mess and move on. Get back to business."

Then suddenly, Hicks shouts, "SOLOMON! What are you doing in this hall?"

I realize I've had my eyes squeezed shut, trying to be invisible. But now they snap open. And I find that I'm looking directly at Solomon, who is standing outside the conference room on the opposite side. From where he's standing, he's looking straight over my head at Hicks and Ennis. And he can see me plain as day. He stares at me, an expression of shock on his face.

Trey once told me Solomon is a snitch, so my heart basically stops, knowing he's about to rat me out. And to the interim principal no less.

Solomon blinks and then looks up, over my head at Mr. Ennis and Hicks.

"I just finished up moving the boxes from your old office to the new office," Solomon says. He walks the length of the window but doesn't look at me again. "I wanted to see if there was anything else you needed me to do before I left."

I don't dare breathe, but my heart unsticks from my ribs and starts to beat again. I can't believe he didn't snitch.

"Ah, thank you, m'boy. In fact, there is one last thing you can do. Mrs. Hall is here to collect the last of her things. There are a few boxes in the main lobby that Mr. Reggie left there for her. She should be arriving any minute if you'd go and take care of that. After that, you're free to leave."

"Got it."

Solomon walks right past me, but doesn't look my way again. When he's out of earshot, Hicks says, "One of the good ones."

Then he and Mr. Ennis are walking through the doors to the side lot, the rest of their conversation taken outside with them.

I gradually breathe again, then crab-walk over to the door, staying low. They're gone. I quickly scurry out of the conference room and down the opposite hall, my phone already in my hand texting Trey.

> Ennis seemed on edge. He was talking to Hicks. Didn't seem to be too bent outta shape on Moore tho. It was all business. They talked about the Promise Fund. Think he might be your guy?

EMAIL RECEIVED BY J.B., TREY & RAMÓN

Sender: darkgamble@anonmail.com
To: J.B., Trey, Ramón

I saw you. I saw you murderers skulking around the school. What are you looking for? Pretty soon the police will nail all three of you. Stay away, or you'll be sorry.

Nobody

This is the part I hate, but also the part I love. When I walk into a room, and no one remembers my name. There's a comfort in being nobody.

You risk nothing, you lose nothing. A lifetime of risk has taught me that it doesn't matter how low you fly—as long as you don't hit the ground. Too high—too much of anything: smiling, frowning, sleeping, moving—and people start to notice. I prefer to fly under the radar.

I'm perfect for a place like Promise, and I recognize that not many are. Here, inside Promise, it's easy to be invisible.

People don't mind asking you to do things when you're nobody. Because even when you do what they ask, they still don't see you as a somebody. You're just another part of the machine to them. You are the printer, you are the pen, you are the keyboard, you are the phone. You are even a video camera.

Eventually people forget you're there, see you the way they would see a lamp. They say things in front of you without thought. They show their hand.

You see everything, even the things they don't mean for you to see. What they don't want you to see.

As nobody, you are used to blending in. You excel at disappearing into the gray paint. You could stand inside a high school, panning down the hallway with camera in hand, recording footage of the newly hung banners, some of them with paint still shining wet. In the background is the roar of the gymnasium, filled with teenagers, all of them becoming somebodies in each other's presence, in this rare period of permissible noise and joy.

Then everyone heads into the gym, the door closes, and you are once again alone, a nobody surrounded by no one. You walk backward down the empty hallway, imagining you had a chance to show more creativity in how *you* see Promise. This is your favorite way to experience school. It's almost as if it's in safe mode. No one looking. Everyone engaged. No one pretending to remember your name.

And then the roar of voices. Two of them, shouting, you don't know from where. Then there they are, square in your eyeline. Two men. One Black, one white. Cursing, swearing. They argue.

If only you had your camera.

Then there's the gun. You immediately turn away at the sight. But you hear it let loose. The bigness of the shot, the way it filled up the whole hall, seemed to crack the ceiling.

You don't have to run. You know how to disappear. You fade into a doorway. There one minute, gone the next. You see the white man come out of the office, but he doesn't see you. He hurries away. He goes into the stairway across from the office.

"There you are! Just the man I came to see!"

Inside, I jump. Outside, I swivel calmly in the office chair to face the counter, where Stanley Ennis is leaning on his elbows, dress shirtsleeves rolled up. He's grinning like a salesman. He always smiles at me like this, and I always wonder what he thinks he's selling me. I know he doesn't actually care if I like him. These rich guys don't usually have to care about stuff like that.

"Hi, Mr. Ennis."

"You've got us all ready for the memorial service tomorrow? Everything queued up?"

I nod.

"Yes, sir, for the most part. Putting the finishing touches on things now."

"You have the new highlights from the last game? Of course we want it to look tasteful. No need to show off at the man's memorial."

"Yes, sir. It looks great. I can send it to you in advance if you'd like to see."

His smile grows wider. Ah, this is what he was after. Always pushing people to do what he wants.

"That would be fantastic! Can I send you any notes I have? I promise it won't be last minute."

"Sure, Mr. Ennis."

"You're a champ." He grins.

I am the computer. I am the camera. I am the desk. I am a phone.

But, I also have a phone. When it vibrates in my pocket, I wait until Mr. Ennis grins his way out of the door to check.

Trey. Another somebody they've tried to make a nobody.

Hey Omar. We just received some bugged out email. You didn't tell anyone we came to the school did you?

I stare at the message for a long time before I answer.

No, I reply eventually. My heart should be beating fast. But I feel a strange calmness. Like I'm sitting inside a sandcastle watching the tide come in. It's inevitable.

I still can't believe they think I killed Moore. I'm almost offended by it, but I also want to laugh. I don't though. Considering what they've been up against, no wonder they're desperate to figure it all out. For the first time, regret claws at me. I should've said something when I realized Moore wasn't handling school funds the proper way. Am I a coward?

But I'm a nobody, who'd listen?

And even if they did listen, even if I became a somebody for a brief moment, why would they believe me without proof? And who knows what type of danger I'd be putting myself in?

The real murderer could come for me next.

CHAPTER TWENTY-FOUR

Revelations

RAMÓN

I can't shake that email I received from the killer. It has to be from the killer.

Not because I'm afraid, but something about the email seemed familiar to me. It's almost like I could hear their voice coming through the computer, but I can't quite make out who it is. In all honesty, whoever sent it seemed desperate, which must mean we're getting closer to the truth.

I decide to send a text to the group to see what's what.

Ramón: Trey and J.B., y'all get a weird email?

Trey: Yea. Gotta be someone still at the school. Ennis was there for game day.

Keyana: J.B. says he wishes he'd seen something.

I think back to Omar, trying to remember if I saw anybody stand out, anybody that was looking our way, but I come up short.

> **Magda:** So it seems like with the email, plus the conversation Brandon overheard with Ennis and Hicks, and the Promise Fund stuff that Omar mentioned, Ennis is our guy.

> **Luis:** Moore must've done something to go back on their arrangement, so Ennis got rid of him.

> **Keyana:** I said it early on, follow the money. So now, how do we nail him?

What we need is hard proof. But it's not like some video footage is going to magically appear after the cops have been searching for so long.

Hold up. Maybe the security cameras at Promise didn't spot anything, but what if someone got video of the game?

Then it comes to me: I remember Omar saying he planned to interview Principal Moore on camera right before he was shot. I shoot him a text.

> **Ramón:** Omar, did you end up getting any footage of Moore the day of the shooting?

Omar: No I never even set up the camera, had some trouble with my mic.

Ramón: You think your mic picked up anything?

Omar: Hmm, I don't think so, but I'll check.

Disappointed, I put my phone down and lie back on the bed. It was worth a shot to ask Omar, but obviously it was too good to be true.

I think about everything that's happened and how upside down my life has become. I think about my days at Promise and those last couple days at school, before Moore was killed. He was spiraling out of control, that's why he treated me, J.B., and Trey that way. It wasn't because of us.

And then it hits me. We aren't bad kids, Moore was just a bad man. This whole time I've been thinking I did something wrong or I made some mistake, but that couldn't be further from the truth. Moore was dealing with his own shit.

But then, another thought hits me and I shoot up in the bed as if a jolt of electricity shoots through me. I remember why that email feels so familiar to me.

CHAPTER TWENTY-FIVE

The Sting

J.B.

Keyana might be the smartest girl I've evet met, and I can't tell if it's because she remembers every single thing she sees, or because her brain is constantly creating new stuff. Either way, I'm pretty sure they're both signs of a genius. There's no way this plan would ever have existed if it wasn't for her, and Omar I guess. But mostly Keyana. And that's exactly what I tell her while we're standing behind Rocky's store, waiting for the others to show up before Moore's memorial.

"I know," she agrees, smiling that cute smile. But then she gets serious, looking me dead in my eyes. "But I need to know one thing. Would you do this for me? If I was up against something like this, would you pull out all the stops to help me?"

I stare at her as hard as I can, so she can feel my eyes pouring into hers.

"When all this is over, I'm going to write you a poem that tells you everything I would do in this world for you. But for right now I'll just say this, I would hoist the whole planet up on my back and carry it around the sun, if you so much as whispered for me to do it."

I can tell by the way her eyes warm up that she believes me. I want to kiss her right there, even while I'm sweating and my nose feels like it might bleed, but then Ramón and the others show up, all with hats on and hoodies up.

We are definitely in disguise.

"So," Keyana says. "We've got some options. We've got Promise uniforms, of course. Which, Luis, if you're going in, I think you should probably opt for that. Magda, I recommend you wear the dress. I'm going to put on the Mercy uniform, if that's cool with you. The point is, we mostly don't want any associations being made between who we are and where we actually fit in. Just in case we catch someone's eye. Luis, you're kind of the exception, for you it should look like it's just another day, you know?"

"So, what," Trey says, raising an eyebrow. "I'm supposed to dress up like a butler or something? Like they do in the movies?"

"Not exactly." She laughs and a thrill jolts through me at the warm sound. "For you and J.B. and Ramón, I borrowed suits from my dad and my brother. I think it's best if people see you as members of the community who've come to pay respects. Even better if they see a suit and assume you're grown."

"Ain't nobody going to believe Ramón is grown," Luis teases, pushing his friend.

"And, uh, no shade, but I don't think any of these suits are going to fit me," I say, eyeing the garment bags.

She smirks at me, and holds one aloft.

"Nice try," Keyana says. "But my dad is 6′5″. Hope you don't mind sharkskin."

"I'm going to be out here looking like an OG," I groan.

"Good. That's the point of disguises, so people think you're something you're not."

We all take turns changing behind the dumpsters in the alley in the back of Rocky's. Better than what usually probably goes down here.

Keyana looks cute in the Mercy uniform, but nothing looks better than her usual tight pants, huge shirt, and hoop earrings. She has her own style and I love that about her.

"You sure Omar is going to come through today?" Trey asks me once we all finish changing. Magda stands there in the floral dress that's too big.

"He said he was just putting on the finishing touches," Ramón says.

"He better not back out last minute. I wish we didn't need to risk getting in trouble today," Trey says.

"I don't know, man. I mean, technically it's not like we're banned from school grounds. We're just suspended from school. The memorial is public," Ramón responds.

"Yeah, so why are we putting on disguises then?"

"Just a precaution," Keyana says. "No unnecessary attention! Let's focus on the task at hand. We may be exonerating you all today."

I check my phone and see it's 11:45; we decide it's time. I wasn't nervous until just now.

"I hope I don't get in trouble for cutting school," Magda mutters.

"Yeah, me neither," says Luis.

Keyana does a double take.

"Wait, Luis why *did* you cut school? We're going to *your* school. You could've just gone into the gymnasium with your class and we'd see you there."

He blinks at her, then shrugs. "I just didn't wanna miss anything."

We all laugh at that. God, what a day. Then Ramón looks at me.

"You're sure that basement door is gonna be open?"

"I picked it when Keyana and I broke into Omar's locker," I say.

"Yeah, but they probably make sure it's kept shut now," Ramón says.

"You'd think," Trey says. He holds up his phone. "But my boy Brandon checked this morning, and it's still unlocked."

"Okay, so we'll all go in the basement door and then we'll split up," Keyana says. She turns to me with big eyes. "But listen. If it seems risky and there's anybody looking or whatever . . . then bail. Okay? Do *not* go in if it's going to be bad. Because it's not even worth it. We can meet up after and—"

I plant a kiss on her lips in front of everybody. By now I know how she gets. Sometimes she's all bugged out and she needs to be stopped before she gets too worked up. She smiles up at me.

"I got it," I say.

"You got it," she agrees.

"We got it," Trey chants, like it's a basketball game, and Luis takes it up too. We all laugh. We've heard them at games. This time, though, nobody says *I promise*. We know by now what good those are.

We stream in silently through the basement door and immediately all go in different directions. I can't stop thinking about what Omar has for us. Today *needs* to go right. But I don't want to get my hopes up.

I can hear the distant sounds of crowds moving through the school—it feels like game day, when the halls of Promise are allowed to be talked in, laughed in. The unfairness of it suddenly hits me. Why does it have to be like this? I'm not a bad guy. None of us are. So why do I have to go all day without even smiling?

Even if my name is cleared, I don't think I ever want to come back to this place. It would be just like going to jail. What's the difference at this point?

I make my way alone down the hall, and all the memories of that day come flooding back. Asking for permission to go to the bathroom and not knowing if I'd actually be allowed to go and piss. Even then, with permission, Hicks stopping me and interrogating me. Going down to the bathroom, trying to have one moment where I'm not being stared at by teachers just waiting for me to put one eyelash out of line.

I hadn't realized it until just now, but these past few days since the murder, being out of school and out from under constant surveillance, are the most relaxed I've been in as long as I can remember. This can't be normal, man. It just can't be.

And from now on, it won't.

CHAPTER TWENTY-SIX

Almost Showtime

TREY

It feels weird to be in the gym again, especially because I'm wearing a suit instead of being suited up to play. The only thing I can think about is the game I should've played that Moore screwed me out of—the one that would have absolutely launched my path toward playing in college.

As I move through the crowd, aiming for the rows and rows of chairs they've got lined up on the gym floor, I can't help but feel those feelings all over again—the rage, the disappointment, the embarrassment. It makes no sense that one single person can have that much control over another person's future.

I choose a seat in the sea of chairs, looking up at the stage where Dean Hicks and Mr. Ennis and other rich people are all lined up. My body floods with anger, seeing them up there, looking all polished, being celebrated while I'm the one suspected of murder.

I take a deep breath and try to stay focused. Me and Ramón and the others all came in separately, drifting away from each other in the crowd. No one notices us. At least, not as far as I can tell. This is the first time I've ever been inside my own school and not felt like I was walking on eggshells. Which is funny because I'm literally here *sneaking in*.

At twelve o'clock on the dot, Hicks rises eagerly from his chair and moves toward the lectern. Behind him, the huge projector screen ripples, and when he greets the audience, a hush falls over the chatter.

"It's wonderful to see so many faces here to celebrate the life of my colleague and—truly—my good friend, Kenneth Moore. Everyone here knows the impact he had on every room he entered, and it does the heart good to see a room *this* big filled up with the evidence of that impact. Surely we are all here in reverence of all he accomplished . . ."

I've been to hella funerals and I always have to make myself stay awake. Not because I'm bored, but because it always feels so insincere. Some folks get uncomfortable when people get up there and cry, snot dripping, but I prefer that, honestly, even if I don't feel that way about the person who died. Because it feels like it's coming from a real place.

When Hicks finishes his stuffy speech, others get up and tell stories about Mr. Moore. All the people lined up on the stage in their suits and shiny shoes are there to speak on his memory. But nobody cries, and all the stories have the same tone: *good ole Kenneth Moore*. Or *you may not always agree with him, but you can't argue that he . . . !*

All of a sudden, I just want to get out of here. Even if it means I have to walk past that huge-ass portrait of Principal Moore that's hanging in the lobby. No reason that painting needed to be that big. More and more, this all just feels like a bunch of egos swimming in a shark tank.

Mr. Ennis takes the mic next. He's dressed up like always. I saw his wife somewhere in the crowd too—fancy pantsuit like she's running for president, or like he is.

"I just want to echo what everyone so far has said," he booms into the mic. "Promise is a special place and it's all thanks to Kenneth Moore."

I glance around the gym, for the first time wondering if the rest of the student body is thinking what I'm thinking—that yeah, Promise *is* a special place thanks to Moore . . . a specially fucked-up place. I catch sight of Ramón and a deep frown is etched across his face.

"I wanted to take this opportunity to announce a big change to Promise as we celebrate this man's life—going forward, this school will be officially renamed as Kenneth Moore Promise Preparatory. We thought it only fitting that as Principal Moore is no longer with us in the flesh, that the school bears his name so that we may always carry the promise of his mission in our hearts."

He keeps speaking, but I just sit there feeling sort of hollow at this announcement. Naming the school after Moore? I mean, big deal. It's just a name. It's just a school. But as I listen to all the people around me clapping and nodding, one thought just comes to my head in a heavy block: *It's not fair.*

It's just not fair.

It makes me sound like a little kid—throwing a fit because I fouled out in a game or something. But it's not fair. The guy who made all of us so miserable and strutted around this place getting in kids' faces and yelling and smelling like alcohol . . . *that* dude gets to shuffle into the afterlife with everyone telling all these bullshit stories about him and putting his name on buildings?

And what about us? Me and J.B. and Ramón? The stories being told about us will never be engraved in gold.

I sigh so loud that the woman next to me shifts. The applause is dying down, and now Hicks is back at the mic. How long do they want to hear themselves *talk*?

"Now it is my pleasure to announce some student speakers," Hicks says, "who wanted to share some final words for their beloved leader . . ."

My heart races as I search the crowd, looking for Omar. Where is he? This plan won't work without him. I had a feeling he'd ditch us although I hoped for otherwise.

Then, right as I go to text the team to abort the mission, I spot him sitting in the very back of the stage, perched like a thin bird. He has a way of just disappearing into the chair, into the crowd. He makes himself unnoticeable somehow. Just melts right past the eye. But right now I can see him, and he's looking at me. We give each other a nod.

Almost showtime.

CHAPTER TWENTY-SEVEN

Grand Finale

RAMÓN

Someone must've noticed me. And after that, there's no holding back the tide.

Promise boys are elite at texting without being noticed, and I know word gets around quick—*They're here*. It's not just students. Invisible nudges are issued, silent pointing fingers. *They're here. The three boys they think did it. There are murderers—or at the very least one—in our midst.*

I try to ignore them all. I keep my eyes on the stage, where I've been staring this whole time. It all feels like such a masquerade.

I'm considering getting up and leaving when Trey texts the group chat:

> We're almost there, grand finale coming real soon.

I suddenly feel like my chair is molten lava, melding me to it, unable to move.

It's not like we're breaking any laws. The cops didn't ban us from this building. But with a crowd here to mourn a man we're suspected of killing, this will get uncomfortable very quickly.

Trey doesn't write back, and I'm afraid to look in his direction. I can feel more eyes on me, crawling like roaches. I'm also afraid of what Trey must be feeling. Knowing that he's the one who brought the weapon into the school. Of all of us, he looks the guiltiest.

Becca is on stage giving a speech about how inspired she was by Moore during his life, and how thanks to him, she's going to be a principal too. *Pfft*, of course she is. I feel for the students she thinks she's saving.

"Who knows," Becca says with that smile she always has on when she knows someone is watching, "maybe one day I'll be principal of Promise!"

For the first time throughout this whole clown show, I hear a couple chuckles from the audience. Antonio from ESL is one of them—I would know his whistle-nose laugh anywhere. It makes me want to laugh too, and so does the look on Hicks's face. He can't snap off on us here the way he would during the school day. There's news cameras here, for God's sake. But he scans the audience with a deadly look, warning us all with the promise of later viciousness.

Another text comes in from Trey:

Heads up, y'all. Here come Mr. Reggie.

Sure enough, Mr. Reggie is moving from the front of the gym in a straight line toward the back, his eyes scanning the chairs. He must have gotten word that we were here. I lower my head and I know the others do too. Out of the corner of my eye, I can see him zeroing in on Trey. That figures—Trey's always the one that people remember as the "bad kid" just because he's always clowning. I imagine them using it against him in court and it makes my stomach turn.

"And for our final student speaker . . . ," Hicks is saying and it stops

Mr. Reggie in his path. He loiters near the gym wall, squinting into the audience. Trey has his face turned toward me, just the right angle to go unseen by Mr. Reggie. I can tell Mr. Reggie's frustrated—he's not about to interrupt the memorial service by making a scene, and then have it be some other dude. I know the suit is throwing him off, and I give an internal hat tip to Keyana.

"It is my pleasure to announce Omar Rosario, a student worker and also Promise's amateur photographer and videographer. You may have noticed the looping videos and stills on all our school's monitors—if you did, then you have seen the fine work of this student! We have him to thank for today's video honoring Principal Moore's life. I have seen it myself, and trust me, there won't be a dry eye in the house."

He welcomes Omar to the lectern with a sweep of his arm, and for the first time, the entire student body sees this kid.

I've seen him a thousand times, of course, almost always in the office. Every time I've gotten detention, it was Omar who gave me my signed slip in the office. Always mumbling an answer when I said thanks, never saying more than necessary. He was in ESL with me for one year, but moved on quickly. I never knew if he was supposed to be in there at the beginning or not—if he just got shunted in there by Moore because he speaks Spanish, or if he just learned English really fast. Who knows.

Omar is usually a mystery, but today he walks up to the mic, tall and straight, with ever so slightly hunched shoulders. His thin hands grasp the mic, adjusting it to reach his mouth.

"Hello," he says to the gym. He doesn't mumble. His voice is soft but clear. "My name is Omar Rosario, and I'd like to thank Principal Hicks for my introduction, as well as the opportunities he and Promise have provided me, allowing me to explore my interests in photography and videography while working toward graduation. I hope everyone here enjoys the film, and I'm sorry it got a little long. It was very difficult to choose which scenes to include and which to cut."

The lights dim on cue, and when I glance at Trey, I see he no longer has to hide his face from Mr. Reggie—the dark does it for him, and Mr. Reggie isn't looking at him anymore anyway. Everyone is gazing up at the big glowing screen. Omar has returned to his seat on the stage and looks politely down at his hands as the video starts to play.

It begins with Promise as it originally looked—pretty much the same, but a little newer, a little shinier. There were a lot more posters then: clubs and organizations and stuff. And there's Moore, walking down the hallway grinning, his hair a lot less gray and his suit a lot less fly. Someone must have had this footage on an old phone—it lacks resolution and the volume isn't crisp. But it's him. And honestly, I might have liked him back then.

Mrs. Hall walks next to him, beaming. There are even shots of him entering classrooms and cutting it up a little bit. All the boys are still dressed in starchy uniforms, but their faces aren't starched the same way. People look a little more relaxed, there are even shots of them talking in the hall. I notice with a start that there's no blue line on the floor. When had that been introduced? You hear people laughing, and you *don't* hear the *beep beep beep* of endless demerits.

As the film progresses, it's like watching a time lapse. Students getting older, smiles getting smaller, the halls getting less cluttered with students and posters. The walls seem to get grayer. There was a period of time before Hicks arrived, and then suddenly he's there—serious shots of the two men moving down the hallway, deep in conversation. Shots of them leaning over paperwork on conference table, posed almost like architects.

I glance up at Hicks and his face is clouded with emotion. His friendship with Moore blooming right here before everyone's eyes. It would make me sad if I didn't know how they backed each other up, but never us. How sometimes it seemed like they would sit in Moore's office and come up with new ways to make us stiff and silent.

Ennis appears in some of these shots, and he always smiles broadly every time he shows up on screen. Omar is kind of a brilliant film-maker, I start to notice—the way he never has a clip of Ennis in the foreground. He's always in the background, chatting or watching or smiling. Because that's who he is at Promise: the behind-the-scenes guy, the man with the money, the guy who whispers in the ear of the guy at the wheel. He gets older too as the film goes on, another testament to Omar's talent: It's all chronological, and it's not so much a sizzle reel of Moore's career, but a history of Promise from past to present.

Then there's me. I catch a glimpse of myself in the background of a cafeteria shot, smiling as I dish someone a pupusa. Did anyone else see me? I'm afraid to glance around. Did Omar include that shot on purpose?

Then there's Moore in the hallway, and he looks the way he did in the days leading up to his murder. Slightly disheveled in his fancy suit. Walking stiffly down the hallway. It's a long shot—he's far from the camera but you can hear him shouting at boys in the halls. I glance at Hicks, and he's frowning.

Then there's J.B.—the camera just pans past him, as if happening to catch him deep in thought. He closes his locker, then walks quietly down the blue line.

Moore again—slamming a dude's locker closed after a kid removes his books. The kid jumps. You can hear some muffled groans in the crowd.

Then there's Trey—pulling up for a three-pointer on the basketball court, laughing entirely too loud, his eyes lit up with a joke. Moore wasn't even in that shot. What was Omar doing? I glance again at the stage, and see Ennis leaning over to speak to Hicks, who is shaking his head.

Then the gym fills with noise. Game day. Banners. Colors. Shouting and cheering and chanting. The hallways flood with people. The camera mills through them like a bird—dodging this way and that way. It's the feeling of being in a crowd, buoyed up by the energy and excitement. Shots from the top of the bleachers, taking in the packed gym. Shots from the doorway, capturing the fast-moving feet of both teams, down and back, down and back. Shots from the hallway, the banner over the gym door that says WE PROMISE.

Then the camera is moving smoothly down the hallway, backward, like being pulled through time. Slow at first, then faster, all the lockers blurring. Somewhere in the distance you can still hear the gym roaring.

The shouting gradually drops down in volume, then rises again, not a blur of many voices but the sharp punctuation of two as the screen goes black.

But the audio continues.

"All you had to do was cut me in, Ken! Could I have made it any clearer? I warned you and now we're here!"

"I told your ass it's not happening! How many ways do I have to tell you no?"

The first voice suddenly fills with hatred, transforming it into something beastly. "You think I'm going to just sit here and watch you keep me out? I can handle it. You think I can't? I handle every other fucking thing you throw my way."

"It takes time to build this and you want to butt your way right in to the top. That's not how this works. And if you had minded your fucking business instead of sticking your nose where it doesn't belong, this wouldn't be a conversation! So if you're mad, you made yourself mad."

They get angrier and angrier, and one of them gets louder, the other trying to quiet him. I know who I'm hearing—their voices clear as day.

Hicks and Moore.

"You think I'm going to let you just . . . not cut me in? Knowing what I know?" Hicks shouts.

"I'm telling you that you don't have a fucking choice in the matter."

There's a momentary pause and you can hear some shuffling noises.

"Oh, you son of a bitch, I fucking dare you!" Moore barks. "I fucking dare you!"

"Cut me in! I know the Promise Fund is just your piggie bank, Kenny! All that money from Ennis going right into your pocket! Cut me in!"

"I said NO!"

When the gun goes off, everyone in the Stanley Ennis Gymnasium gasps. Wilson Hicks, the dean of students, now interim principal, caught on tape murdering his partner in crime, Principal Moore.

My abuela always says I have a skill for picking up on vibes. The email J.B., Trey, and me received was the giveaway. *Skulking*, Hicks said. He had used that word with me before.

The tape keeps playing and we hear the body of Principal Kenneth Moore fall to the floor. We hear rustling around the room, scrambling as if trying to wipe fingerprints, set the scene. And then, all we hear is silence.

Keyana Glenn

On stage, Wilson Hicks is scrambling to turn on the mic, to make the presentation stop. He's frantic. Meanwhile, Omar Rosario sits calmly in his chair with his hands folded in his lap.

In the audience people are shouting. Some people are jumping on the phone to call the police but they don't need to—the cops are already here. I saw them when we snuck in with the other attendees. Big events like these always have cops at them, and today is no different.

Nobody knows what to do, and I don't either. I'm just sitting in the chair, wishing I was sitting next to J.B., whose face looks like it did in Omar's film—serious, thoughtful, studious, even while everyone else is bugging out.

"Everyone stay seated!" Hicks shouts. "We're going to figure this out. We're going to figure out what happened here. Some kind of sick practical joke . . . he will be expelled . . ."

Everyone seems frozen.

Except the Promise Boys.

It's J.B. first. While Hicks is shouting at everyone to stay seated, stay silent, J.B. slowly stands up from his folding chair. You can't miss him. All 6'3" of him, standing there in my father's suit, doing nothing, arms by his sides. He just stands, staring up at Hicks. Everyone sees him, and the whispers surge. Some of them aren't whispers.

He's innocent. That's J.B. Williamson. He's innocent.

Then it's Trey. He stands up too, the suit hanging off his shoulders a little.

Trey Jackson. He's here too. Trey didn't do it.

Then Ramón. He's trembling as he stands—I can see him from here.

Ramón Zambrano. He's innocent. They're all innocent.

One by one, the Promise Boys stand up. They say nothing. But one after another, row after row, the other students stand, until every single uniform in the gym is standing, straight-backed, in defiance.

And finally, Omar Rosario stands too.

KENNETH MOORE'S HOMICIDE CASE

DCPD OFFICIAL REPORT

Further interrogations and collection of both physical and digital evidence indicates that Kenneth Moore, late principal of Urban Promise Prep, led a years-long fraud and embezzlement scheme involving donor and political funds. Stanley Ennis, Lindsay Ennis, and one other board member were also implicated. Investigations are forthcoming–Detective Ash will be pursuing the Ennis case with a team of three.

Irrefutable evidence points to Wilson Hicks, former dean of the student body at Urban Promise Prep, as being responsible for the death of Moore. Charges include murder, coercion, blackmail, falsification of evidence, misconduct, and evidence tampering. The murder weapon was found in Hicks's home. The gun carried fingerprints belonging to Hicks.

When faced with audio of the tape recorded by student Omar Rosario, Hicks admits to confronting Moore about his embezzlement, and to pressuring Moore to share the funds. Hicks seems willing to provide information about others involved in the scheme–we will consult with the Associate District Attorney as matters proceed.

Lab reports confirmed J.B. Williamson's claim that the blood on his shirt was his own–in fact, witnesses report

Williamson's nose started bleeding in the gymnasium at Promise Prep the day the Rosario video was shown.

Trey Jackson's guardian, Terrance Jackson, confirms the gun is his and that he hadn't known it was missing—records indicate that he has not attended a shooting range in many months, supporting his claim of no knowledge. Hicks admits that he found the gun in the bathroom when doing an inspection in search of contraband. Exactly how the gun got there is unknown but it is believed the weapon may have been stolen from Mr. Jackson.

On the part of Ramón Zambrano, Hicks had initially claimed that his fingerprints were on the young man's hairbrush found at the scene of the murder because he'd picked it up when he discovered the body. But after further interrogation, Hicks admitted that he stole the brush from the school's office and planted it in Moore's office.

This investigation finds all three Promise Boys—J.B. Williamson, Trey Jackson, and Ramón Zambrano—innocent.

THE PROMISE PREP PAPER

BY MARCUS WATTS,
EDITOR IN CHIEF

One year after the murder of Principal Kenneth Moore shook our close-knit community, Promise Preparatory, now newly renamed, is thriving under the leadership of Principal Carla Hall. A visitor to this school might not recognize it from one year ago, as the hallways are now filled with noise, as well as posters for events and newly formed organizations, including this newspaper, which has already won an award for its integrity and excellence.

The events of last year required a massive reorganization of everything from values to the handbook to staff. You might only recognize a handful of teachers—Principal Hall was meticulous as she shifted everything about Promise. There is now a student government, as well as six mental health advisors, a full ESL staff, and a sensory room that the student body refers to as the Chill Mansion.

The student-led Research Committee has found that these are the measures a truly successful school environment requires. When their research uncovers a new endeavor that the committee believes might best serve the Promise student body, they propose it to Principal Hall, who then meets with student government. These are just some of the new additions at Promise, but many aspects of Moore's tenure have been removed. Including the blue line.

On this day, one year after proving the innocence of three Promise alumni who were accused of murdering former Principal Moore, the *Promise Prep Paper* thought it appropriate to shine a light on the paths of these young men who, though no longer students here, carry on the new legacy of what this school believes in and stands for.

Ramón Zambrano, founder of the SCI program here at Promise—which remains one of the most popular and well-regarded programs in the district—received a full ride to the Sullivan School of Culinary Arts, where he is preparing for a career as a chef.

Trey Jackson graduated as the top-scoring senior in the district and now plays basketball at the D1 level, majoring in computer science.

And J.B. Williamson is on a year-long road trip with his high school sweetheart, Keyana Glenn. They deferred college for a year—she, law; he, musical composition—while they explore the country together.

The lives of these three young men follow their unique paths, but wherever they go, the student body at Promise Prep applauds them for their courage, and for embodying the tenets of the Promise motto, which may be a little different since the last time you heard it:

We are the young men of Promise Prep.
We are destined for greatness.
We deserve joy.
We are extraordinary.
We ask from the world what we give to the world:
respect, wisdom, and grace.
We are each other's hope.
We are responsible for our futures.
We are the future.

We promise

Acknowledgments

As always, first and foremost I want to thank the best teammate I could ever have, my darling wife. You are my rock! Thank you to my beautiful twin baby girls, my parents, my in-laws, and all my extended relatives and friends for supporting me through my journey. Thank you for pouring into me so that I may pour into my art.

Thank you, Brian Geffen, for championing *Promise Boys* and shepherding this process as elegantly as anything I've ever seen. Your dedication has been inspiring. Your insight and creative brain have been invaluable, and I could not have told this story without you.

Thank you, Dhonielle Clayton, who believed in me enough to give me the shot I've always needed. Thank you for sharing your wisdom and expertise so willingly and being a mentor to so many voices in this industry. I'm forever grateful.

Thank you, Joanna Volpe, for being the BOSS you are! Thank you for standing in my corner and being there whenever I need you. And thank you to the rest of the teams at New Leaf and Cake Creative for your support behind-the-scenes, especially Jenniea Carter, Jordan Hill, Meredith Barnes, Shelly Romero, Clay Morrell, and Carlyn Greenwald.

Thank you to the rest of the publishing team at Macmillan—Carina

Licon, Ann Marie Wong, Jean Feiwel, Jennifer Besser, Rich Deas, Kat Kopit, Alexei Esikoff, Veronica Ambrose, Ryan Jenkins, Jennifer Edwards, Kristin Dulaney, Sam Smith, and Emma Jones. Much, much love to the brilliant publicity and marketing team—Molly Ellis, Morgan Rath, Mariel Dawson, Melissa Zar, Katie Quinn, Naheid Shahsamand, Mary Van Akin, and Kristen Luby. And a special shout-out of gratitude to Ken Nwadiogbu, who created our phenomenal book cover.

Without you all, *Promise Boys* could not be possible. This has been such a great community of smart, talented people who believe in the power of storytelling.

And lastly, but certainly not least, I want to thank all the students I've ever taught, or passed in a hallway, or coached in Little League. You all have inspired me in so many ways and I'm working to return the favor. I want to thank the young ones reading this book today—you can be anything in this world you want to be. Your imagination is one of your biggest assets; take advantage!

With much love, thank you all.

—Nick